DOVER·THRIFT·EDITIONS

Henry V

WILLIAM SHAKESPEARE

DOVER PUBLICATIONS, INC.
Mineola, New York

DOVER THRIFT EDITIONS

GENERAL EDITOR: PAUL NEGRI
EDITOR OF THIS VOLUME: T. N. R. ROGERS

Copyright

Theatrical Rights

This Dover Thrift Edition may be used in its entirety, in adaptation, or in any other way for theatrical productions, professional and amateur, in the United States, without fee, permission, or acknowledgment. (This may not apply outside of the United States, as copyright conditions may vary.)

Bibliographical Note

This Dover edition, first published in 2003, contains the unabridged text of *The Life of King Henry V* as published in Volume XIII of *The Caxton Edition of the Complete Works of William Shakespeare*, Caxton Publishing Company, London, n.d. We have revised the explanatory footnotes from the Caxton edition, added new footnotes, and prepared a new introductory Note especially for this edition.

Library of Congress Cataloging-in-Publication Data

Shakespeare, William, 1564–1616.
 Henry V / William Shakespeare.
  p. cm.
 ISBN-13: 978-0-486-42887-1
 ISBN-10: 0-486-42887-7
  1. Henry V, King of England, 1387–1422—Drama. 2. Great Britain—History—Henry V, 1413–1422—Drama. I. Title: Henry the Fifth. II. Title.

PR2812 .A1 2003
822.3'3—dc21

2002037090

Manufactured in the United States by Courier Corporation
42887705
www.doverpublications.com

Note

BY THE TIME depicted in this play, Henry has left his riotous youth behind, discarded his drinking companions from the Boar's-Head Tavern, and become a great leader. Though he has retained his common touch and his sense of humor, he has become fiercely focused, brave, modest, and forgiving—but with a sense of justice so strong that when one of his former companions robs a church in France he does not hesitate to have him put to death. He has become the greatest of English kings.

This, at least, was the Elizabethans' estimation of Henry V. The last decade of the sixteenth century, when Shakespeare wrote his history plays, was a time of intense patriotism in England. People had strong memories of the Spanish Armada's bold incursion, in July 1588, into the English Channel, with the intent—fully supported and blessed by the Pope—of deposing Elizabeth and installing a Catholic ruler in her stead. The Armada's defeat was even more earth-shaking than Henry V's unforgettably lopsided victory at Agincourt; it marked the end of Spanish dominance and the rise of England as a world power. In the exuberant patriotism of the following decade, Shakespeare's history plays (which are among the earliest plays he wrote) proved to be resoundingly popular. The first part of *Henry VI* probably was staged the year after the Armada's defeat, when the author was only twenty-five, and he kept the franchise going through the 1590s, following the remaining two parts of *Henry VI* with *Richard III, Richard II, King John,* and the two parts of *Henry IV* before tackling *Henry V. Henry V* was first performed in 1599 and has remained one of the most popular of Shakespeare's history plays ever since.

The historical Henry V was probably quite different from the man Shakespeare portrays. As far as we can tell, he was never the slacker or tavern habitué portrayed in *Henry IV*. Even as a teen-ager, he was in the heart of battles and politics. At least nominally, he was administrator of Wales from the age of thirteen. Three years later, he was in actual command of the English forces in the battle of Shrewsbury. Even during his memorable though relatively brief kingship,[1] Henry was not

[1] Two years after marrying Catherine, when their son (the future Henry VI) was eight months old, Henry, who was longing to mount a new crusade to the Holy Land, died in France of dysentery. He was not quite thirty-five years old. Catherine, who was twenty-one at the time, went on to bear five children to her Welsh squire, Owen Tudor (who may or may not have become her husband); the eldest of these children, Edmund, later fathered Henry VII, the first in the Tudor line that was to end with Elizabeth.

entirely the sort of person portrayed by Shakespeare. He was acknowl-
edged to be brave, honorable, and just, but he could also be ruthless,
intolerant, and fanatic. As a modern biographer has written, "Henry
had none of the more attractive virtues—he had little charm, although
a real concern for his soldiers; no sense of humor, and a truly terrifying
conviction of his own position as the instrument of God."[2]

But Shakespeare did not have access to modern scholarship, and actually he stayed fairly close to the sources that were available to him—
primarily Raphael Holinshed's *Chronicles of England, Scotland, and
Ireland* (published in 1577) and Samuel Daniel's poem *The Civile
Wars Between the Two Houses of Lancaster and Yorke* (1595). He also
picked up a few incidents (such as the Dauphin's gift of tennis balls,
Pistol's encounter with Monsieur le Fer, and Henry's wooing of
Catherine) from the anonymous chronicle play *The Famous Victories
of Henry V* (probably first acted around 1588). These works all acceded
to the view of Henry's wild youth and sudden conversion that was first
promulgated about twenty years after his death—a view that seems to
have had its origin in the friendship that the young Henry had had with
Sir John Oldcastle.[3] Oldcastle was a leader of the Lollards (who had the
misfortune to espouse protestantism a hundred years before Henry VIII
gave it the royal imprimatur), and when Prince Hal became king he
signed his old friend's death warrant. Though Sir John had paid for his
religious beliefs by being burned to death over a slow fire, he was still
remembered as a corrupter of youth.

All these historical facts are interesting. But what matters, when you
read this play, is not what the "real" Henry V was like, or what
Shakespeare's sources said, or what became of Catherine, or any of the
other ribbons and bows that, in the guise of introductions or critiques,
one can wrap around any of Shakespeare's works. The only important
thing is the play itself. Transport yourself into the "wooden O" of the
Globe theater in 1499, and find yourself being pulled along inexorably
by the astounding dramaturgy, poetry, passion, humor, and human
truth that make up this and virtually every other play by Will.
Shakespeare, Gent.

---

[2]Margaret Wade Labarge, in *Henry V: The Cautious Conqueror* (London: Secker and
Warburg, 1975).
[3]Shakespeare originally gave Oldcastle's name to the character who later turned into
Jack Falstaff. He evidently changed the name at the behest of one of Oldcastle's de-
scendants.

Contents

Dramatis Personæ[1]

KING HENRY the Fifth.
DUKE OF GLOUCESTER,
DUKE OF BEDFORD, } brothers to the King.
DUKE OF EXETER, uncle to the King.
DUKE OF YORK, cousin to the King.
EARLS OF SALISBURY, WESTMORELAND, and WARWICK.
ARCHBISHOP OF CANTERBURY.
BISHOP OF ELY.
EARL OF CAMBRIDGE.
LORD SCROOP.
SIR THOMAS GREY.
SIR THOMAS ERPINGHAM, GOWER, FLUELLEN, MACMORRIS, JAMY, officers
 in King Henry's army.
BATES, COURT, WILLIAMS, soldiers in the same.
PISTOL, NYM, BARDOLPH.
Boy.
A Herald.

CHARLES the Sixth, King of France.
LEWIS, the Dauphin.
DUKES OF BURGUNDY, ORLEANS, and BOURBON.
The Constable of France.
RAMBURES AND GRANDPRÉ, French Lords.
Governor of Harfleur.
MONTJOY, a French Herald.
Ambassadors to the King of England.

ISABEL, Queen of France.
KATHARINE, daughter to Charles and Isabel.
ALICE, a lady attending on her.
Hostess of a tavern in Eastcheap, formerly Mistress Quickly, and now
 married to Pistol.

Lords, Ladies, Officers, Soldiers, Citizens, Messengers, and Attendants.

Chorus.

SCENE—*England; afterwards France*

---

[1]The full text of this play first appeared in the First Folio of 1623. An imperfect sketch
was issued surreptitiously in 1600 in a Quarto volume, which was reissued in 1602 and
1608. The First Folio divides the piece into Acts only, although the opening heading
runs "Actus Primus Scœna Prima." Pope first supplied scenic subdivisions.

PROLOGUE

Enter Chorus

CHORUS.   O for a muse of fire, that would ascend
   The brightest heaven of invention,
   A kingdom for a stage, princes to act
   And monarchs to behold the swelling scene!
   Then should the warlike Harry, like himself,
   Assume the port of Mars; and at his heels,
   Leash'd in like hounds, should famine, sword and fire
   Crouch for employment. But pardon, gentles all,
   The flat unraised spirits that have dared
   On this unworthy scaffold to bring forth   10
   So great an object: can this cockpit hold
   The vasty fields of France? or may we cram
   Within this wooden O the very casques
   That did affright the air at Agincourt?
   O, pardon! since a crooked figure may
   Attest in little place a million;
   And let us, ciphers to this great accompt,
   On your imaginary forces work.
   Suppose within the girdle of these walls
   Are now confined two mighty monarchies,   20
   Whose high upreared and abutting fronts

---

6 *port*] carriage.
9 *unraised*] humble, lowly.
10 *scaffold*] stage.
11 *cockpit*] place appointed for cock-fighting matches, a reference to the confined area
   of the theatre.
13 *this wooden O*] A reference to the newly-erected Globe Theatre with its circular in-
   terior. This play was one of the first pieces produced there.
   casques] helmets.
17 *accompt*] account.
18 *imaginary forces*] powers of imagination.
21 *abutting fronts*] the cliffs of Dover and Calais.

1

The perilous narrow ocean parts asunder:
Piece out our imperfections with your thoughts;
Into a thousand parts divide one man,
And make imaginary puissance;
Think, when we talk of horses, that you see them
Printing their proud hoofs i' the receiving earth;
For 't is your thoughts that now must deck our kings,
Carry them here and there; jumping o'er times,
Turning the accomplishment of many years   30
Into an hour-glass: for the which supply,
Admit me Chorus to this history;
Who prologue-like your humble patience pray,
Gently to hear, kindly to judge, our play.

                                                     [*Exit.*

---

23 *Piece out*] Make up.
24 *Into a thousand . . . man*] Suppose one man to represent a thousand.
25 *puissance*] armed might, army.
31 *an hour-glass*] A rough estimate of the time occupied by a theatrical performance.
32 *Chorus*] Interpreter.

ACT I.

SCENE I. *London. An Ante-Chamber in the King's Palace.*

Enter the ARCHBISHOP of CANTERBURY, *and the* BISHOP of ELY

CANTERBURY.   My Lord, I'll tell you; that self bill is urged,
 Which in the eleventh year of the last king's reign
 Was like, and had indeed against us pass'd,
 But that the scambling and unquiet time
 Did push it out of farther question.
ELY.   But how, my lord, shall we resist it now?
CANT.   It must be thought on. If it pass against us,
 We lose the better half of our possession:
 For all the temporal lands, which men devout
 By testament have given to the church,   10
 Would they strip from us; being valued thus:
 As much as would maintain, to the king's honour,
 Full fifteen earls and fifteen hundred knights,
 Six thousand and two hundred good esquires;
 And, to relief of lazars and weak age,
 Of indigent faint souls past corporal toil,
 A hundred almshouses right well supplied;
 And to the coffers of the king beside,
 A thousand pounds by the year: thus runs the bill.
ELY.   This would drink deep.   20
CANT.   'T would drink the cup and all.
ELY.   But what prevention?
CANT.   The king is full of grace and fair regard.
ELY.   And a true lover of the holy church.

 1 CANTERBURY] The speaker is Henry Chichele, Archbishop of Canterbury, founder of
 All Souls College, Oxford. Shakespeare makes him the leader of the plot against
 Henry IV's bill for confiscating church property.
  self] same.
 4 *scambling*] bustling, turbulent.
 15 *lazars*] lepers.

3

CANT.   The courses of his youth promised it not.
   The breath no sooner left his father's body,
   But that his wildness, mortified in him,
   Seem'd to die too; yea, at that very moment,
   Consideration like an angel came
   And whipp'd the offending Adam out of him,   30
   Leaving his body as a paradise,
   To envelope and contain celestial spirits.
   Never was such a sudden scholar made;
   Never came reformation in a flood,
   With such a heady currance, scouring faults;
   Nor never Hydra-headed wilfulness
   So soon did lose his seat, and all at once,
   As in this king.
ELY.   We are blessed in the change,
CANT.   Hear him but reason in divinity,   40
   And all-admiring with an inward wish
   You would desire the king were made a prelate:
   Hear him debate of commonwealth affairs,
   You would say it hath been all in all his study:
   List his discourse of war, and you shall hear
   A fearful battle render'd you in music:
   Turn him to any cause of policy,
   The Gordian knot of it he will unloose,
   Familiar as his garter: that, when he speaks,
   The air, a charter'd libertine, is still,   50
   And the mute wonder lurketh in men's ears,
   To steal his sweet and honey'd sentences;
   So that the art and practic part of life
   Must be the mistress to this theoric:
   Which is a wonder how his grace should glean it,
   Since his addiction was to courses vain,
   His companies unletter'd, rude and shallow,

27 *mortified*] killed.
29 *Consideration*] Reflection, repentance.
30 *offending Adam*] original sin.
35 *heady currance*] impetuous flow.
36 *Hydra-headed wilfulness*] many headed, infinitely varied, waywardness.
37 *his seat*] throne.
42 *prelate*] a high-ranking church dignitary.
47 *cause of policy*] question of state affairs.
53 *art and practic part of life*] practical experience of life.
54 *mistress to this theoric*] the inspirer or teacher of this theoretical knowledge.
57 *companies*] companions, associates.

His hours fill'd up with riots, banquets, sports,
And never noted in him any study,
Any retirement, any sequestration   60
From open haunts and popularity.
ELY. The strawberry grows underneath the nettle,
And wholesome berries thrive and ripen best
Neighbour'd by fruit of baser quality:
And so the prince obscured his contemplation
Under the veil of wildness; which, no doubt,
Grew like the summer grass, fastest by night,
Unseen, yet crescive in his faculty.
CANT. It must be so; for miracles are ceased;
And therefore we must needs admit the means   70
How things are perfected.
ELY.   But, my good lord,
How now for mitigation of this bill
Urged by the commons? Doth his majesty
Incline to it, or no?
CANT.   He seems indifferent,
Or rather swaying more upon our part
Than cherishing the exhibiters against us;
For I have made an offer to his majesty,
Upon our spiritual convocation   80
And in regard of causes now in hand,
Which I have open'd to his grace at large,
As touching France, to give a greater sum
Than ever at one time the clergy yet
Did to his predecessors part withal.
ELY. How did this offer seem received, my lord?
CANT. With good acceptance of his majesty;
Save that there was not time enough to hear,
As I perceived his grace would fain have done,
The severals and unhidden passages   90
Of his true titles to some certain dukedoms,
And generally to the crown and seat of France,
Derived from Edward, his great-grandfather.
ELY. What was the impediment that broke this off?
CANT. The French ambassador upon that instant

61 *popularity*] intercourse with the common people.
65 *obscured his contemplation*] concealed his devotion to study.
68 *crescive in his faculty*] increasing in strength.
77 *swaying*] inclining.
90 *The severals . . . passages*] The details and clear or undoubted steps in the lineage.

Craved audience; and the hour, I think, is come
To give him hearing: is it four o'clock?
ELY. It is.
CANT. Then go we in, to know his embassy;
    Which I could with a ready guess declare,   100
    Before the Frenchman speak a word of it.
ELY. I'll wait upon you, and I long to hear it.   [*Exeunt.*

SCENE II. *The Same—The Presence Chamber.*

Enter KING HENRY, GLOUCESTER, BEDFORD, EXETER, WARWICK,
    WESTMORELAND, *and* Attendants

K. HEN. Where is my gracious Lord of Canterbury?
EXE. Not here in presence.
K. HEN.   Send for him, good uncle.
WEST. Shall we call in the ambassador, my liege?
K. HEN. Not yet, my cousin: we would be resolved,
    Before we hear him, of some things of weight
    That task our thoughts, concerning us and France.

Enter the ARCHBISHOP of CANTERBURY *and the* BISHOP of ELY

CANT. God and his angels guard your sacred throne
    And make you long become it!
K. HEN.   Sure, we thank you.   10
    My learned lord, we pray you to proceed
    And justly and religiously unfold
    Why the law Salique that they have in France
    Or should, or should not, bar us in our claim:
    And God forbid, my dear and faithful lord,
    That you should fashion, wrest, or bow your reading,
    Or nicely charge your understanding soul
    With opening titles miscreate, whose right
    Suits not in native colours with the truth;
    For God doth know how many now in health   20
    Shall drop their blood in approbation
    Of what your reverence shall incite us to.

5 *resolved*] satisfied.
13 *the law Salique*] the Salic law against the succession of females.
17 *nicely charge . . . soul*] by subtlety or sophistry oppress or injure your conscience,
    which knows the truth.
18 *With . . . miscreate*] By setting forth spurious titles.
21–22 *in approbation Of*] in making good, in actively carrying out.

Therefore take heed how you impawn our person,
How you awake our sleeping sword of war:
We charge you, in the name of God, take heed;
For never two such kingdoms did contend
Without much fall of blood; whose guiltless drops
Are every one a woe, a sore complaint
'Gainst him whose wrongs give edge unto the swords
That make such waste in brief mortality.   30
Under this conjuration speak, my lord;
For we will hear, note and believe in heart
That what you speak is in your conscience wash'd
As pure as sin with baptism.
CANT.   Then hear me, gracious sovereign, and you peers,
That owe yourselves, your lives and services
To this imperial throne. There is no bar
To make against your highness' claim to France
But this, which they produce from Pharamond,
"In terram Salicam mulieres ne succedant":   40
"No woman shall succeed in Salique land":
Which Salique land the French unjustly gloze
To be the realm of France, and Pharamond
The founder of this law and female bar.
Yet their own authors faithfully affirm
That the land Salique is in Germany,
Between the floods of Sala and of Elbe;
Where Charles the Great, having subdued the Saxons,
There left behind and settled certain French;
Who, holding in disdain the German women   50
For some dishonest manners of their life,
Establish'd then this law; to wit, no female
Should be inheritrix in Salique land:
Which Salique, as I said, 'twixt Elbe and Sala,
Is at this day in Germany call'd Meisen.
Then doth it well appear the Salique law
Was not devised for the realm of France;
Nor did the French possess the Salique land
Until four hundred one and twenty years
After defunction of King Pharamond,   60
Idly supposed the founder of this law;
Who died within the year of our redemption

42 *gloze*] explain, interpret.
51 *dishonest*] unchaste.
60 *defunction*] death of.

Four hundred twenty-six; and Charles the Great
Subdued the Saxons, and did seat the French
Beyond the river Sala, in the year
Eight hundred five. Besides, their writers say,
King Pepin, which deposed Childeric,
Did, as heir general, being descended
Of Blithild, which was daughter to King Clothair,
Make claim and title to the crown of France. 70
Hugh Capet also, who usurp'd the crown
Of Charles the duke of Lorraine, sole heir male
Of the true line and stock of Charles the Great,
To find his title with some shows of truth,
Though, in pure truth, it was corrupt and naught,
Convey'd himself as heir to the Lady Lingare,
Daughter to Charlemain, who was the son
To Lewis the emperor, and Lewis the son
Of Charles the Great. Also King Lewis the tenth,
Who was sole heir to the usurper Capet, 80
Could not keep quiet in his conscience,
Wearing the crown of France, till satisfied
That fair Queen Isabel, his grandmother,
Was lineal of the Lady Ermengare,
Daughter to Charles the foresaid duke of Lorraine:
By the which marriage the line of Charles the Great
Was re-united to the crown of France.
So that, as clear as is the summer's sun,
King Pepin's title and Hugh Capet's claim,
King Lewis his satisfaction, all appear 90
To hold in right and title of the female:
So do the kings of France unto this day;
Howbeit they would hold up this Salique law
To bar your highness claiming from the female,
And rather choose to hide them in a net
Than amply to imbar their crooked titles
Usurp'd from you and your progenitors.
K. HEN.   May I with right and conscience make this claim?
CANT.   The sin upon my head, dread sovereign!

76 *Convey'd himself*] Represented himself, passed himself off.
84 *lineal of*] lineally descended from.
90 *King Lewis his satisfaction*] the satisfying of King Lewis's scruples.
95 *hide them in a net*] hide the weakness of their argument in a tangle of contradictions.
96 *amply to imbar . . . titles*] fully and frankly to admit the fatal defect in (and so disown)
   their own unjust or false titles.

For in the book of Numbers is it writ,   100
When the man dies, let the inheritance
Descend unto the daughter. Gracious lord,
Stand for your own; unwind your bloody flag;
Look back into your mighty ancestors:
Go, my dread lord, to your great-grandsire's tomb,
From whom you claim; invoke his warlike spirit,
And your great-uncle's, Edward the Black Prince,
Who on the French ground play'd a tragedy,
Making defeat on the full power of France,
Whiles his most mighty father on a hill   110
Stood smiling to behold his lion's whelp
Forage in blood of French nobility.
O noble English, that could entertain
With half their forces the full pride of France
And let another half stand laughing by,
All out of work and cold for action!

ELY.   Awake remembrance of these valiant dead,
And with your puissant arm renew their feats:
You are their heir; you sit upon their throne;
The blood and courage that renowned them   120
Runs in your veins; and my thrice-puissant liege
Is in the very May-morn of his youth,
Ripe for exploits and mighty enterprises.

EXE.   Your brother kings and monarchs of the earth
Do all expect that you should rouse yourself,
As did the former lions of your blood.

WEST.   They know your grace hath cause and means and might;
So hath your highness; never king of England
Had nobles richer and more loyal subjects,
Whose hearts have left their bodies here in England   130
And lie pavilion'd in the fields of France.

CANT.   O, let their bodies follow, my dear liege,
With blood and sword and fire to win your right;
In aid whereof we of the spiritualty
Will raise your highness such a mighty sum
As never did the clergy at one time
Bring in to any of your ancestors.

---

103 *your bloody flag*] your flag of war.
108 *Who . . . play'd a tragedy*] A reference to the battle of Crécy in 1346.
116 *cold for action*] cold for want of action, for standing idle.
131 *And lie pavilion'd*] And are already (in imagination) dwelling in tents in preparation
for war.
134 *spiritualty*] clergy.

K. HEN. We must not only arm to invade the French,
     But lay down our proportions to defend
     Against the Scot, who will make road upon us   140
     With all advantages.
CANT. They of those marches, gracious sovereign,
     Shall be a wall sufficient to defend
     Our inland from the pilfering borderers.
K. HEN. We do not mean the coursing snatchers only,
     But fear the main intendment of the Scot,
     Who hath been still a giddy neighbour to us;
     For you shall read that my great-grandfather
     Never went with his forces into France,
     But that the Scot on his unfurnish'd kingdom   150
     Came pouring, like the tide into a breach,
     With ample and brim fulness of his force,
     Galling the gleaned land with hot assays,
     Girding with grievous siege castles and towns;
     That England, being empty of defence,
     Hath shook and trembled at the ill neighbourhood.
CANT. She hath been then more fear'd than harm'd, my liege;
     For hear her but exampled by herself:
     When all her chivalry hath been in France,
     And she a mourning widow of her nobles,   160
     She hath herself not only well defended,
     But taken and impounded as a stray
     The King of Scots; whom she did send to France,
     To fill King Edward's fame with prisoner kings,
     And make her chronicle as rich with praise,
     As is the ooze and bottom of the sea
     With sunken wreck and sumless treasuries.
WEST. But there's a saying very old and true,
      "If that you will France win,
      Then with Scotland first begin":   170
     For once the eagle England being in prey,

139 *lay down our proportions*] allocate our forces.
140 *make road . . . advantages*] make inroads at every favorable opportunity.
142 *They of those marches*] The inhabitants of the Scottish border.
145 *coursing snatchers*] scattered, unattached raiders.
146 *the main intendment of the Scot*] the design of the armed forces of Scotland.
147 *giddy*] fickle, untrustworthy.
153 *assays*] assaults.
163 *The King of Scots*] David II, the king of Scotland, was taken prisoner at the battle of
    Neville's Cross, October 17, 1346, and was captive in England for eleven years.
164 *prisoner kings*] John II, king of France, was also one of Edward III's prisoners.

To her unguarded nest the weasel Scot
Comes sneaking and so sucks her princely eggs,
Playing the mouse in absence of the cat,
To tear and havoc more than she can eat.
EXE. It follows then the cat must stay at home:
Yet that is but a crush'd necessity,
Since we have locks to safeguard necessaries,
And pretty traps to catch the petty thieves.
While that the armed hand doth fight abroad,   180
The advised head defends itself at home;
For government, though high and low and lower,
Put into parts, doth keep in one consent,
Congreeing in a full and natural close,
Like music.
CANT. Therefore doth heaven divide
The state of man in divers functions,
Setting endeavour in continual motion;
To which is fixed, as an aim or butt,
Obedience: for so work the honey-bees,   190
Creatures that by a rule in nature teach
The act of order to a peopled kingdom.
They have a king and officers of sorts;
Where some, like magistrates correct at home,
Others, like merchants, venture trade abroad,
Others, like soldiers, armed in their stings,
Make boot upon the summer's velvet buds,
Which pillage they with merry march bring home
To the tent-royal of their emperor;
Who, busied in his majesty, surveys   200
The singing masons building roofs of gold,
The civil citizens kneading up the honey,
The poor mechanic porters crowding in
Their heavy burdens at his narrow gate,
The sad-eyed justice, with his surly hum,

177 *a crush'd necessity*] a need or condition that is put out of account or rendered
    negligible.
181 *advised*] thoughtful.
183 *in one consent*] in unison.
184 *Congreeing . . . close*] Harmonizing . . . cadence.
189 *butt*] goal or target.
197 *boot*] booty, prey.
202 *civil*] orderly.
205 *sad-eyed*] grave-eyed.

Delivering o'er to executors pale
The lazy yawning drone. I this infer,
That many things, having full reference
To one consent, may work contrariously:
As many arrows, loosed several ways,   210
Come to one mark; as many ways meet in one town;
As many fresh streams meet in one salt sea;
As many lines close in the dial's centre;
So may a thousand actions, once afoot,
End in one purpose, and be all well borne
Without defeat. Therefore to France, my liege.
Divide your happy England into four;
Whereof take you one quarter into France,
And you withal shall make all Gallia shake.
If we, with thrice such powers left at home,   220
Cannot defend our own doors from the dog,
Let us be worried and our nation lose
The name of hardiness and policy.
K. HEN.   Call in the messengers sent from the Dauphin.
                                               [Exeunt some Attendants.
Now are we well resolved; and, by God's help,
And yours, the noble sinews of our power,
France being ours, we'll bend it to our awe,
Or break it all to pieces: or there we'll sit,
Ruling in large and ample empery
O'er France and all her almost kingly dukedoms,   230
Or lay these bones in an unworthy urn,
Tombless, with no remembrance over them:
Either our history shall with full mouth
Speak freely of our acts, or else our grave,
Like Turkish mute, shall have a tongueless mouth,
Not worshipp'd with a waxen epitaph.

Enter Ambassadors *of France*

206 *executors*] executioners.
219 *Gallia*] France.
223 *hardiness and policy*] valor and political wisdom.
224 *Dauphin*] the heir apparent to the French throne.
229 *empery*] dominion.
236 *Not worshipp'd with . . . epitaph*] Not honored even with an inscription in wax.
   "Waxen" suggests that which can be easily effaced, is not lasting.

Now are we well prepared to know the pleasure
Of our fair cousin Dauphin; for we hear
Your greeting is from him, not from the king.
FIRST AMB.   May't please your majesty to give us leave   240
Freely to render what we have in charge;
Or shall we sparingly show you far off
The Dauphin's meaning and our embassy?
K. HEN.   We are no tyrant, but a Christian king;
Unto whose grace our passion is as subject
As are our wretches fetter'd in our prisons:
Therefore with frank and with uncurbed plainness
Tell us the Dauphin's mind.
FIRST AMB.   Thus, then, in few.
Your highness, lately sending into France,   250
Did claim some certain dukedoms, in the right
Of your great predecessor, King Edward the third.
In answer of which claim, the prince our master
Says that you savour too much of your youth,
And bids you be advised there's nought in France
That can be with a nimble galliard won;
You cannot revel into dukedoms there.
He therefore sends you, meeter for your spirit,
This tun of pleasure; and, in lieu of this,
Desires you let the dukedoms that you claim   260
Hear no more of you. This the Dauphin speaks.
K. HEN.   What treasure, uncle?
EXE.   Tennis-balls, my liege.
K. HEN.   We are glad the Dauphin is so pleasant with us;
His present and your pains we thank you for:
When we have match'd our rackets to these balls,
We will, in France, by God's grace, play a set
Shall strike his father's crown into the hazard.
Tell him he hath made a match with such a wrangler
That all the courts of France will be disturb'd   270

256 *galliard*] quick dance.
258 *meeter*] more fitting.
259 *This tun*] This barrel.
    in lieu of this] in exchange for this gift.
267 *play a set*] This play abounds in the technical vocabulary of a game or set at tennis.
268 *the hazard*] a hole in the wall of the tennis court near the ground. A stroke into this
    hole would score a point for the player.
269 *a wrangler*] an opponent.

With chaces. And we understand him well,
How he comes o'er us with our wilder days,
Not measuring what use we made of them.
We never valued this poor seat of England;
And therefore, living hence, did give ourself
To barbarous license; as 't is ever common
That men are merriest when they are from home.
But tell the Dauphin I will keep my state,
Be like a king and show my sail of greatness
When I do rouse me in my throne of France: 280
For that I have laid by my majesty,
And plodded like a man for working-days;
But I will rise there with so full a glory
That I will dazzle all the eyes of France,
Yea, strike the Dauphin blind to look on us.
And tell the pleasant prince this mock of his
Hath turn'd his balls to gun-stones; and his soul
Shall stand sore charged for the wasteful vengeance
That shall fly with them: for many a thousand widows
Shall this his mock mock out of their dear husbands; 290
Mock mothers from their sons, mock castles down;
And some are yet ungotten and unborn
That shall have cause to curse the Dauphin's scorn.
But this lies all within the will of God,
To whom I do appeal; and in whose name
Tell you the Dauphin I am coming on,
To venge me as I may and to put forth
My rightful hand in a well-hallow'd cause.
So get you hence in peace; and tell the Dauphin
His jest will savour but of shallow wit, 300
When thousands weep more than did laugh at it.
Convey them with safe conduct. Fare you well.
                              [*Exeunt* Ambassadors.
EXE.   This was a merry message.
K. HEN.   We hope to make the sender blush at it.

271 *chaces*] the word has various meanings in tennis, viz., a double bounce or an un-
    successful return.
272 *comes o'er us*] taunts us.
274 *seat of England*] throne of England.
275 *hence*] away from the court.
281 *For that I have laid by*] Despite the fact that I have laid aside or neglected my
    dignity.
287 *gun-stones*] cannonballs, which were originally made of stone.
288 *sore charged*] sorely burdened with responsibility.

Therefore, my lords, omit no happy hour
That may give furtherance to our expedition;
For we have now no thought in us but France,
Save those to God, that run before our business.
Therefore let our proportions for these wars
Be soon collected, and all things thought upon   310
That may with reasonable swiftness add
More feathers to our wings; for, God before,
We'll chide this Dauphin at his father's door.
Therefore let every man now task his thought,
That this fair action may on foot be brought.
                              [*Exeunt. Flourish.*

309 *proportions*] numbers.
312 *God before*] God guiding us.

ACT II. — PROLOGUE

Enter Chorus

CHORUS.   Now all the youth of England are on fire,
    And silken dalliance in the wardrobe lies:
    Now thrive the armorers, and honour's thought
    Reigns solely in the breast of every man:
    They sell the pasture now to buy the horse,
    Following the mirror of all Christian kings,
    With winged heels, as English Mercuries.
    For now sits Expectation in the air,
    And hides a sword from hilts unto the point
    With crowns imperial, crowns and coronets,   10
    Promised to Harry and his followers.
    The French, advised by good intelligence
    Of this most dreadful preparation,
    Shake in their fear and with pale policy
    Seek to divert the English purposes.
    O England! model to thy inward greatness,
    Like little body with a mighty heart,
    What mightst thou do, that honour would thee do,
    Were all thy children kind and natural!
    But see thy fault! France hath in thee found out   20
    A nest of hollow bosoms, which he fills
    With treacherous crowns; and three corrupted men,
    One, Richard Earl of Cambridge, and the second,
    Henry Lord Scroop of Masham, and the third,
    Sir Thomas Gray, knight, of Northumberland,
    Have, for the gilt of France, — O guilt indeed! —
    Confirm'd conspiracy with fearful France;

2 *silken dalliance*] silk clothes (i.e., luxuries) and idle pleasures are stored away.
16 *model*] model in miniature, pattern.
19 *kind*] filial.
20 *France*] The king of France.

16

And by their hands this grace of kings must die,
If hell and treason hold their promises,
Ere he take ship for France, and in Southampton.   30
Linger your patience on; and we'll digest
The abuse of distance; force a play:
The sum is paid; the traitors are agreed;
The king is set from London; and the scene
Is now transported, gentles, to Southampton;
There is the playhouse now, there must you sit:
And thence to France shall we convey you safe,
And bring you back, charming the narrow seas
To give you gentle pass; for, if we may,
We'll not offend one stomach with our play.   40
But, till the king come forth, and not till then,
Unto Southampton do we shift our scene.

                                                 [*Exit.*

SCENE I. *London. A Street.*

Enter Corporal NYM *and* Lieutenant BARDOLPH

BARD.   Well met, Corporal Nym.

NYM.   Good morrow, Lieutenant Bardolph.

BARD.   What, are Ancient Pistol and you friends yet?

NYM.   For my part, I care not: I say little; but when time shall
serve, there shall be smiles; but that shall be as it may. I dare
not fight; but I will wink and hold out mine iron: it is a simple one; but what though? it will toast cheese, and it will endure cold as another man's sword will: and there's an end.

BARD.   I will bestow a breakfast to make you friends; and we'll be

---

31–32 *Linger . . . on . . . force a play*] The meaning may be, "Prolong your patience, and
    we'll set right the awkwardness of the distance between the different places where the
    incidents of the play occur, and compel the sequence of events into the necessary lim-
    its of dramatic action."

40 *We'll not offend one stomach*] We'll make nobody seasick.

41–42 *But, till the king . . . scene*] The words very crudely explain that the scene will not
    be shifted from London to Southampton until the king comes onstage again.

---

1 *Nym*] In thieves' language the word is a verb meaning "to steal."

3 *Ancient*] Ensign.

5 *when time . . . smiles*] probably Nym means that one of them will have the laugh on
    his side, when the time comes for him and Pistol to square accounts.

6 *wink*] shut my eyes.

  iron] sword.

    all three sworn brothers to France: let it be so, good Corporal   10
    Nym.

NYM.   Faith, I will live so long as I may, that's the certain of it;
    and when I cannot live any longer, I will do as I may: that is
    my rest, that is the rendezvous of it.

BARD.   It is certain, corporal, that he is married to Nell Quickly:
    and, certainly, she did you wrong; for you were troth-plight
    to her.

NYM.   I cannot tell: things must be as they may: men may sleep,
    and they may have their throats about them at that time; and
    some say knives have edges. It must be as it may: though pa-   20
    tience be a tired mare, yet she will plod. There must be con-
    clusions. Well, I cannot tell.

Enter PISTOL *and* HOSTESS

BARD.   Here comes Ancient Pistol and his wife: good corporal,
    be patient here. How now, mine host Pistol!

PIST.   Base tike, call'st thou me host?
    Now, by this hand, I swear, I scorn the term;
    Nor shall my Nell keep lodgers.

HOST.   No, by my troth, not long; for we cannot lodge and board
    a dozen or fourteen gentlewomen that live honestly by the
    prick of their needles, but it will be thought we keep a bawdy   30
    house straight. [NYM *and* PISTOL *draw.*] O well a day, Lady,
    if he be not drawn now! we shall see wilful adultery and mur-
    der committed.

BARD.   Good lieutenant! good corporal! offer nothing here.

NYM.   Pish!

PIST.   Pish for thee, Iceland dog! thou prick-ear'd cur of Iceland!

HOST.   Good Corporal Nym, show thy valour, and put up your
    sword.

NYM.   Will you shog off? I would have you solus.

PIST.   "Solus," egregious dog? O viper vile!   40

---

10 *sworn brothers to France*] bosom comrades on our visit to France.
14 *rest*] stake or wager; a term in the game of "primero."
16 *troth-plight*] betrothed.
21–22 *conclusions*] an end to all things.
25 *tike*] ugly dog.
34 *offer nothing*] do not fight.
36 *Iceland dog*] a shaggy, sharp-eared, white-haired dog, in much favor with ladies in
    Shakespeare's time.
39 *shog off*] go.
40 *solus*] alone.

The "solus" in thy most mervailous face;
The "solus" in thy teeth, and in thy throat,
And in thy hateful lungs, yea, in thy maw, perdy,
And, which is worse, within thy nasty mouth!
I do retort the "solus" in thy bowels;
For I can take, and Pistol's cock is up,
And flashing fire will follow.

NYM.   I am not Barbason; you cannot conjure me. I have an humour to knock you indifferently well. If you grow foul with
me, Pistol, I will scour you with my rapier, as I may, in fair   50
terms: if you would walk off, I would prick your guts a little,
in good terms, as I may: and that's the humour of it.

PIST.   O braggart vile, and damned furious wight!
The grave doth gape, and doting death is near;
Therefore exhale.

BARD.   Hear me, hear me what I say: he that strikes the first
stroke, I'll run him up to the hilts, as I am a soldier.
                                                        [*Draws.*

PIST.   An oath of mickle might; and fury shall abate.
Give me thy fist, thy fore-foot to me give:
Thy spirits are most tall.   60

NYM.   I will cut thy throat, one time or other, in fair terms: that
is the humour of it.

PIST.   "Couple a gorge!"
That is the word. I thee defy again.
O hound of Crete, think'st thou my spouse to get?
No; to the spital go,
And from the powdering-tub of infamy
Fetch forth the lazar kite of Cressid's kind,

41 *mervailous*] Pistol's affected pronunciation of "marvelous."
43 *perdy*] a corruption of "par Dieu," "by God."
46 *take*] "take fire" or "catch fire"; used of a gun going off. Pistol is talking to himself as
   if he were a pistol.
48 *Barbason*] a popular name of a fiend of hell.
52 *that's the humour of it*] that's my meaning.
53 *wight*] person.
55 *exhale*] draw swords, in Pistol's vocabulary.
58 *mickle*] great.
63 *"Couple a gorge!"*] Corruption of "Coupe la gorge," cut your throat.
65 O *hound of Crete*] Cretan hounds were credited by classical authors with special excellence.
66–67 *spital . . . powdering-tub*] a reference to the hospital and the treatment accorded
   there to sufferers from venereal disease.
68 *the lazar kite of Cressid's kind*] the leprous whore.

Doll Tearsheet she by name, and her espouse:
I have, and I will hold, the quondam Quickly   70
For the only she; and—pauca, there's enough.
Go to.

Enter the Boy

BOY.   Mine host Pistol, you must come to my master, and you,
    hostess: he is very sick, and would to bed. Good Bardolph,
    put thy face between his sheets, and do the office of a
    warming-pan. Faith, he's very ill.
BARD.   Away, you rogue!
HOST.   By my troth, he'll yield the crow a pudding one of these
    days. The king has killed his heart. Good husband, come
    home presently.   [*Exeunt* HOSTESS *and* boy.   80
BARD.   Come, shall I make you two friends? We must to France
    together: why the devil should we keep knives to cut one an-
    other's throats?
PIST.   Let floods o'erswell, and fiends for food howl on!
NYM.   You'll pay me the eight shillings I won of you at betting?
PIST.   Base is the slave that pays.
NYM.   That now I will have: that's the humour of it.
PIST.   As manhood shall compound: push home.   [*They draw.*
BARD.   By this sword, he that makes the first thrust, I'll kill him;
    by this sword, I will.   90
PIST.   Sword is an oath, and oaths must have their course.
BARD.   Corporal Nym, an thou wilt be friends, be friends: an
    thou wilt not, why, then, be enemies with me too. Prithee,
    put up.
NYM.   I shall have my eight shillings I won of you at betting?
PIST.   A noble shalt thou have, and present pay;
    And liquor likewise will I give to thee,
    And friendship shall combine, and brotherhood:
    I'll live by Nym, and Nym shall live by me;
    Is not this just? for I shall sutler be   100

70 *quondam*] former.
71 *pauca*] in brief.
75–76 *do the office of a warming-pan*] A reference to Bardolph's fiery red face.
78 *yield . . . a pudding*] be eaten by crows.
79 *killed*] broken.
88 *As manhood shall compound*] As valor shall settle the issue (in fight).
91 *sword is an oath*] Elizabethans often swore by their swords.
94 *put up*] sheathe thy sword.
96 *A noble*] A coin worth less than eight shillings.
100 *sutler*] one who sells goods to soldiers.

Unto the camp, and profits will accrue.
Give me thy hand.
NYM. I shall have my noble?
PIST. In cash most justly paid.
NYM. Well, then, that's the humour of 't.

Re-enter HOSTESS

HOST. As ever you came of women, come in quickly to Sir
John. Ah, poor heart! he is so shaked of a burning quotidian
tertian, that it is most lamentable to behold. Sweet men,
come to him.
NYM. The king hath run bad humours on the knight; that's the   110
even of it.
PIST. Nym, thou hast spoke the right;
His heart is fracted and corroborate.
NYM. The king is a good king: but it must be as it may; he passes
some humours and careers.
PIST. Let us condole the knight; for, lambkins, we will live.

SCENE II. *Southampton—A Council-Chamber.*

Enter EXETER, BEDFORD, *and* WESTMORELAND

BED. 'Fore God, his grace is bold, to trust these traitors.
EXE. They shall be apprehended by and by.
WEST. How smooth and even they do bear themselves!
As if allegiance in their bosoms sat,
Crowned with faith and constant loyalty.
BED. The king hath note of all that they intend,
By interception which they dream not of.
EXE. Nay, but the man that was his bedfellow,
Whom he hath dull'd and cloy'd with gracious favours,
That he should, for a foreign purse, so sell   10
His sovereign's life to death and treachery.

107–108 *quotidian tertian*] Mrs. Quickly jumbles together two kinds of fever, the "quotidian," in which the paroxysms take place every day, and the "tertian," in which they
take place every third day.
110 *run bad humours*] let loose evil caprices, or perversities of temper.
110–111 *that's the even of it*] that's the level truth.
113 *corroborate*] a blunder for corrupted.
114–115 *he passes . . . careers*] he indulges in some whims and caprices.
116 *lambkins*] term of endearment.

---

9 *dull'd and cloy'd . . . favours*] rendered inappreciative through excess of generosity.

Trumpets sound. Enter KING HENRY, SCROOP, CAMBRIDGE,
    GREY, *and* Attendants

K. HEN.   Now sits the wind fair, and we will aboard.
    My Lord of Cambridge, and my kind Lord of Masham,
    And you, my gentle knight, give me your thoughts:
    Think you not that the powers we bear with us
    Will cut their passage through the force of France,
    Doing the execution and the act
    For which we have in head assembled them?
SCROOP.   No doubt, my liege, if each man do his best.
K. HEN.   I doubt not that; since we are well persuaded   20
    We carry not a heart with us from hence
    That grows not in a fair consent with ours,
    Nor leave not one behind that doth not wish
    Success and conquest to attend on us.
CAM.   Never was monarch better fear'd and loved
    Than is your majesty: there's not, I think, a subject
    That sits in heart-grief and uneasiness
    Under the sweet shade of your government.
GREY.   True: those that were your father's enemies
    Have steep'd their galls in honey, and do serve you   30
    With hearts create of duty and of zeal.
K. HEN.   We therefore have great cause of thankfulness;
    And shall forget the office of our hand,
    Sooner than quittance of desert and merit
    According to the weight and worthiness.
SCROOP.   So service shall with steeled sinews toil,
    And labour shall refresh itself with hope,
    To do your grace incessant services.
K. HEN.   We judge no less. Uncle of Exeter,
    Enlarge the man committed yesterday,   40
    That rail'd against our person: we consider
    It was excess of wine that set him on;
    And on his more advice we pardon him.
SCROOP.   That's mercy, but too much security:
    Let him be punish'd, sovereign, lest example

15 *powers*] armed forces.
18 *in head*] in force.
22 *in a fair consent*] in unison, in friendly concord.
31 *create*] composed, made up.
40 *Enlarge*] Set free.
43 *on his more advice*] on his return to better judgment.
44 *security*] confidence.

Breed, by his sufferance, more of such a kind.
K. HEN.   O, let us yet be merciful.
CAM.   So may your highness, and yet punish too.
GREY.   Sir,
    You show great mercy, if you give him life,   50
    After the taste of much correction.
K. HEN.   Alas, your too much love and care of me
    Are heavy orisons 'gainst this poor wretch!
    If little faults, proceeding on distemper,
    Shall not be wink'd at, how shall we stretch our eye
    When capital crimes, chew'd, swallow'd and digested,
    Appear before us? We'll yet enlarge that man,
    Though Cambridge, Scroop and Grey, in their dear care
    And tender preservation of our person,
    Would have him punish'd. And now to our French causes: 60
    Who are the late commissioners?
CAM.   I one, my lord:
    Your highness bade me ask for it to-day.
SCROOP.   So did you me, my liege.
GREY.   And I, my royal sovereign.
K. HEN.   Then, Richard Earl of Cambridge, there is yours;
    There yours, Lord Scroop of Masham; and, sir knight,
    Grey of Northumberland, this same is yours:
    Read them; and know, I know your worthiness.
    My Lord of Westmoreland, and uncle Exeter,   70
    We will aboard to-night. Why, how now, gentlemen!
    What see you in those papers that you lose
    So much complexion? Look ye, how they change!
    Their cheeks are paper. Why, what read you there,
    That hath so cowarded and chased your blood
    Out of appearance?
CAM.   I do confess my fault;
    And do submit me to your highness' mercy.
GREY. ⎫
SCROOP.⎬To which we all appeal.
      ⎭

---

46 *sufferance*] being pardoned.
53 *orisons*] prayers, pleas.
54 *proceeding on distemper*] resulting from sudden outbursts of passion (in this case from excess of drink).
56 *chew'd . . . digested*] premeditated.
61 *late*] lately or recently appointed.
63 *ask for it*] ask for my warrant as commissioner.

K. HEN.   The mercy that was quick in us but late,   80
    By your own counsel is suppress'd and kill'd:
    You must not dare, for shame, to talk of mercy;
    For your own reasons turn into your bosoms,
    As dogs upon their masters, worrying you.
    See you, my princes and my noble peers,
    These English monsters! My Lord of Cambridge here,
    You know how apt our love was to accord
    To furnish him with all appertinents
    Belonging to his honour; and this man
    Hath, for a few light crowns, lightly conspired,   90
    And sworn unto the practices of France,
    To kill us here in Hampton: to the which
    This knight, no less for bounty bound to us
    Than Cambridge is, hath likewise sworn. But, O,
    What shall I say to thee, Lord Scroop? thou cruel,
    Ingrateful, savage and inhuman creature!
    Thou that didst bear the key of all my counsels,
    That knew'st the very bottom of my soul,
    That almost mightst have coin'd me into gold,
    Wouldst thou have practised on me for thy use,   100
    May it be possible, that foreign hire
    Could out of thee extract one spark of evil
    That might annoy my finger? 't is so strange,
    That, though the truth of it stands off as gross
    As black and white, my eye will scarcely see it.
    Treason and murder ever kept together,
    As two yoke-devils sworn to either's purpose,
    Working so grossly in a natural cause,
    That admiration did not hoop at them:
    But thou, 'gainst all proportion, didst bring in   110

80 *quick*] alive.
87 *accord*] consent.
88 *appertinents*] accessories.
91 *sworn unto the practices*] sworn to engage in the plots.
93 *This knight*] i.e., Grey.
100 *practised on*] plotted against.
104 *stands off as gross*] stands out as palpable.
107 *yoke-devils*] partners in a diabolical cause.
108–109 *Working so grossly in . . . hoop at them*] Working toward a purpose that suits
    them so naturally that they provoked no outcry of wonder.
110 *'gainst all proportion*] against all the fitness of things.

Wonder to wait on treason and on murder:
And whatsoever cunning fiend it was
That wrought upon thee so preposterously
Hath got the voice in hell for excellence:
All other devils that suggest by treasons
Do botch and bungle up damnation
With patches, colours, and with forms being fetch'd
From glistering semblances of piety;
But he that temper'd thee bade thee stand up,
Gave thee no instance why thou shouldst do treason,   120
Unless to dub thee with the name of traitor.
If that same demon that hath gull'd thee thus
Should with his lion gait walk the whole world,
He might return to vasty Tartar back,
And tell the legions "I can never win
A soul so easy as that Englishman's."
O, how hast thou with jealousy infected
The sweetness of affiance! Show men dutiful?
Why, so didst thou: seem they grave and learned?
Why, so didst thou: come they of noble family?   130
Why, so didst thou: seem they religious?
Why, so didst thou: or are they spare in diet,
Free from gross passion or of mirth or anger,
Constant in spirit, not swerving with the blood,
Garnish'd and deck'd in modest complement,
Not working with the eye without the ear,
And but in purged judgement trusting neither?
Such and so finely bolted didst thou seem:
And thus thy fall hath left a kind of blot,

115 *suggest by treasons*] tempt to treasons.
119 *temper'd thee*] fashioned thee.
120 *instance*] reason.
123 *lion gait*] Biblical reference to the Devil, who was said to walk about the world like
     a lion.
124 *Tartar*] Tartarus, the classical name for hell.
128 *affiance*] trust.
134 *blood*] passionate impulse.
135 *complement*] accomplishment.
136 *Not working . . . ear*] Not judging men merely by appearance, but listening to their
     talk.
137 *but*] save, except.
138 *bolted*] refined.

To mark the full-fraught man and best indued　　　　140
With some suspicion. I will weep for thee;
For this revolt of thine, methinks, is like
Another fall of man. Their faults are open:
Arrest them to the answer of the law;
And God acquit them of their practices!

EXE.　　I arrest thee of high treason, by the name of Richard Earl
　　　　of Cambridge.
　　I arrest thee of high treason, by the name of Henry Lord
　　　　Scroop of Masham.
　　I arrest thee of high treason, by the name of Thomas Grey,
　　　　knight, of Northumberland.

SCROOP.　　Our purposes God justly hath discover'd;
　　And I repent my fault more than my death;　　　　150
　　Which I beseech your highness to forgive,
　　Although my body pay the price of it.

CAM.　　For me, the gold of France did not seduce;
　　Although I did admit it as a motive
　　The sooner to effect what I intended:
　　But God be thanked for prevention;
　　Which I in sufferance heartily will rejoice,
　　Beseeching God and you to pardon me.

GREY.　　Never did faithful subject more rejoice
　　At the discovery of most dangerous treason　　　　160
　　Than I do at this hour joy o'er myself,
　　Prevented from a damned enterprise:
　　My fault, but not my body, pardon, sovereign.

K. HEN.　　God quit you in his mercy! Hear your sentence.
　　You have conspired against our royal person,
　　Join'd with an enemy proclaim'd, and from his coffers
　　Received the golden earnest of our death;
　　Wherein you would have sold your king to slaughter,
　　His princes and his peers to servitude,
　　His subjects to oppression and contempt,　　　　170
　　And his whole kingdom into desolation.
　　Touching our person seek we no revenge;

---

140 *the full-fraught man*] the truly virtuous man.
145 *God acquit them*] God absolve them.
155 *The sooner . . . intended*] Cambridge's object was to obtain the English crown for
　　his brother-in-law, Roger Mortimer, Earl of March, a descendant of Edward III.
157 *in sufferance*] in my suffering (for my sin).
167 *the golden earnest*] advance payment.

But we our kingdom's safety must so tender,
Whose ruin you have sought, that to her laws
We do deliver you. Get you therefore hence,
Poor miserable wretches, to your death:
The taste whereof, God of his mercy give
You patience to endure, and true repentance
Of all your dear offences! Bear them hence.
        [*Exeunt* CAMBRIDGE, SCROOP, *and* GREY, *guarded.*
Now, lords, for France; the enterprise whereof   180
Shall be to you, as us, like glorious.
We doubt not of a fair and lucky war,
Since God so graciously hath brought to light
This dangerous treason lurking in our way
To hinder our beginnings. We doubt not now
But every rub is smoothed on our way.
Then forth, dear countrymen: let us deliver
Our puissance into the hand of God,
Putting it straight in expedition.
Cheerly to sea; the signs of war advance: 190
No king of England, if not king of France.   [*Exeunt.*

SCENE III. *London — Before a Tavern.*

Enter PISTOL, HOSTESS, NYM, BARDOLPH, *and* Boy

HOST.   Prithee, honey-sweet husband, let me bring thee to
    Staines.
PIST.   No; for my manly heart doth yearn.
    Bardolph, be blithe: Nym, rouse thy vaunting veins:
    Boy, bristle thy courage up; for Falstaff he is dead,
    And we must yearn therefore.
BARD.   Would I were with him, wheresome'er he is, either in
    heaven or in hell!
HOST.   Nay, sure, he's not in hell: he's in Arthur's bosom, if ever
    man went to Arthur's bosom. A' made a finer end and went   10
    away an it had been any christom child; a' parted even just

179 *dear*] grievous.
186 *rub*] obstacle.
188 *puissance*] army.

---

  1 *bring*] accompany.
  3 *yearn*] mourn.
  9 *in Arthur's bosom*] Mrs. Quickly's blunder for "in Abraham's bosom."
11 *an . . . christom child*] as if he had been a newly christened child.

between twelve and one, even at the turning o' the tide: for
after I saw him fumble with the sheets, and play with flow-
ers, and smile upon his fingers' ends, I knew there was but
one way; for his nose was as sharp as a pen, and a' babbled
of green fields. "How now, Sir John!" quoth I: "what, man!
be o' good cheer." So a' cried out "God, God, God!" three
or four times. Now I, to comfort him, bid him a' should not
think of God; I hoped there was no need to trouble himself
with any such thoughts yet. So a' bade me lay more clothes   20
on his feet: I put my hand into the bed and felt them, and
they were as cold as any stone; then I felt to his knees, and
they were as cold as any stone, and so upward and upward,
and all was as cold as any stone.

NYM.   They say he cried out of sack.

HOST.   Ay, that a' did.

BARD.   And of women.

HOST.   Nay, that a' did not.

BOY.   Yes, that a' did; and said they were devils incarnate.

HOST.   A' could never abide carnation; 't was a colour he never   30
liked.

BOY.   A' said once, the devil would have him about women.

HOST.   A' did in some sort, indeed, handle women; but then he
was rheumatic, and talked of the whore of Babylon.

BOY.   Do you not remember, a' saw a flea stick upon Bardolph's
nose, and a' said it was a black soul burning in hell-fire?

BARD.   Well, the fuel is gone that maintained that fire: that's all
the riches I got in his service.

NYM.   Shall we shog? the king will be gone from Southampton.

PIST.   Come, let's away. My love, give me thy lips.   40
Look to my chattels and my movables:
Let senses rule; the word is "Pitch and Pay":
Trust none;
For oaths are straws, men's faiths are wafer-cakes,
And hold-fast is the only dog, my duck:
Therefore, Caveto be thy counsellor.

25 *cried out of sack*] exclaimed against sack (a Spanish wine).
34 *rheumatic*] her blunder for "lunatic."
37 *fuel*] alcohol.
39 *shog*] be off.
42 "*Pitch and Pay*"] a colloquial phrase for "pay ready money."
45 *hold-fast . . . dog*] Cf. the old proverb "Brag is a good dog, but holdfast a better."
   my duck] my good friend. (A colloquial term of endearment.)
46 *Caveto*] caution.

Go, clear thy crystals. Yoke-fellows in arms,
Let us to France; like horse-leeches, my boys,
To suck, to suck, the very blood to suck!
BOY.   And that's but unwholesome food, they say.   50
PIST.   Touch her soft mouth, and march.
BARD.   Farewell, hostess.   [*Kissing her.*
NYM.   I cannot kiss, that is the humour of it; but, adieu.
PIST.   Let housewifery appear: keep close, I thee command.
HOST.   Farewell; adieu.   [*Exeunt.*

SCENE IV. *France—The King's Palace.*

Flourish. Enter the FRENCH KING, *the* DAUPHIN, *the* DUKES *of*
BERRI *and* BRETAGNE, *the* CONSTABLE, *and others*

FR. KING.   Thus comes the English with full power upon us;
And more than carefully it us concerns
To answer royally in our defences.
Therefore the Dukes of Berri and of Bretagne,
Of Brabant and of Orleans, shall make forth,
And you, Prince Dauphin, with all swift dispatch,
To line and new repair our towns of war
With men of courage and with means defendant;
For England his approaches makes as fierce
As waters to the sucking of a gulf.   10
It fits us then to be as provident
As fear may teach us out of late examples
Left by the fatal and neglected English
Upon our fields.
DAU.   My most redoubted father,
It is most meet we arm us 'gainst the foe;
For peace itself should not so dull a kingdom,
Though war nor no known quarrel were in question,
But that defences, musters, preparations,

47 *clear thy crystals*] dry thine eyes.
54 *keep close*] stay at home.

---

2 *more than carefully*] with more than common care.
7 *line*] support, strengthen.
10 *As waters . . . gulf*] As waters drawn to a whirlpool.
13 *the fatal and neglected English*] the English whom we have fatally neglected (po-
    tentially to our ruin).
16 *most meet*] imperative.
17 *so dull*] make so lazy.

Should be maintain'd, assembled and collected,   20
As were a war in expectation.
Therefore, I say 't is meet we all go forth
To view the sick and feeble parts of France:
And let us do it with no show of fear;
No, with no more than if we heard that England
Were busied with a Whitsun morris-dance:
For, my good liege, she is so idly king'd,
Her sceptre so fantastically borne
By a vain, giddy, shallow, humorous youth,
That fear attends her not.   30

CON.   O peace, Prince Dauphin!
You are too much mistaken in this king:
Question your grace the late ambassadors,
With what great state he heard their embassy,
How well supplied with noble counsellors,
How modest in exception, and withal
How terrible in constant resolution,
And you shall find his vanities forespent
Were but the outside of the Roman Brutus,
Covering discretion with a coat of folly;   40
As gardeners do with ordure hide those roots
That shall first spring and be most delicate.

DAU.   Well, 't is not so, my lord high constable;
But though we think it so, it is no matter:
In cases of defence 't is best to weigh
The enemy more mighty than he seems:
So the proportions of defence are fill'd;
Which of a weak and niggardly projection
Doth, like a miser, spoil his coat with scanting
A little cloth.   50

FR. KING.   Think we King Harry strong;
And, princes, look you strongly arm to meet him.

26 *morris-dance*] A vigorous English dance performed by men in costumes and bells.
29 *humorous*] capricious, frolicsome.
36 *modest in exception*] diffident in expressions of dissent.
    withal] in addition.
39–40 *Brutus . . . folly*] Lucius Junius Brutus, the founder of Republican Rome, according to Livy, feigned idiocy to escape ruin at the hands of his foe, King Tarquinius Superbus, whose rule he ultimately brought to an end.
41 *ordure*] manure.
47 *the proportions*] the appropriate needs.
48 *Which . . . projection*] The provision of which on a weak and inadequate plan. (This clause forms the subject of "doth spoil" in the next line.)

The kindred of him hath been flesh'd upon us;
And he is bred out of that bloody strain
That haunted us in our familiar paths:
Witness our too much memorable shame
When Cressy battle fatally was struck,
And all our princes captived by the hand
Of that black name, Edward, Black Prince of Wales;
Whiles that his mountain sire, on mountain standing,   60
Up in the air, crown'd with the golden sun,
Saw his heroical seed, and smiled to see him,
Mangle the work of nature, and deface
The patterns that by God and by French fathers
Had twenty years been made. This is a stem
Of that victorious stock; and let us fear
The native mightiness and fate of him.

Enter a Messenger

MESS.   Ambassadors from Harry King of England
    Do crave admittance to your majesty.
FR. KING.   We'll give them present audience. Go, and bring
    them.   [*Exeunt* Messenger *and certain* Lords.   70
    You see this chase is hotly follow'd, friends.
Dau.   Turn head, and stop pursuit; for coward dogs
    Most spend their mouths when what they seem to threaten
    Runs far before them. Good my sovereign,
    Take up the English short, and let them know
    Of what a monarchy you are the head:
    Self-love, my liege, is not so vile a sin
    As self-neglecting.

Re-enter Lords, *with* EXETER *and train*

FR. KING.   From our brother England?
EXE.   From him; and thus he greets your majesty.   80
    He wills you, in the name of God Almighty,
    That you divest yourself, and lay apart
    The borrow'd glories that by gift of heaven,

---

53 *The kindred . . . upon us*] His family (Edward III was King Henry's great-grandfather,
    and Edward the Black Prince was his great-uncle) gained its first military experience
    in conflict with us. (A hound was said to be "fleshed," when it first tasted blood in
    the chase.)
57 *Cressy battle*] Crécy, a major defeat for the French in 1346. (See above: I, ii, 108.)
60 *mountain sire*] reference to Edward III, who was born in mountainous Wales.
73 *spend their mouths*] bark their loudest.

By law of nature and of nations, 'long
To him and to his heirs; namely, the crown
And all wide-stretched honours that pertain
By custom and the ordinance of times
Unto the crown of France. That you may know
'T is no sinister nor no awkward claim,
Pick'd from the worm-holes of long-vanish'd days,   90
Nor from the dust of old oblivion raked,
He sends you this most memorable line,
In every branch truly demonstrative;
Willing you overlook this pedigree:
And when you find him evenly derived
From his most famed of famous ancestors,
Edward the third, he bids you then resign
Your crown and kingdom, indirectly held
From him the native and true challenger.

FR. KING.   Or else what follows?   100

EXE.   Bloody constraint; for if you hide the crown
Even in your hearts, there will he rake for it:
Therefore in fierce tempest is he coming,
In thunder and in earthquake, like a Jove,
That, if requiring fail, he will compel;
And bids you, in the bowels of the Lord,
Deliver up the crown, and to take mercy
On the poor souls for whom this hungry war
Opens his vasty jaws; and on your head
Turning the widows' tears, and the orphans' cries,   110
The dead men's blood, the pining maidens' groans,
For husbands, fathers and betrothed lovers,
That shall be swallow'd in this controversy.
This is his claim, his threatening, and my message;
Unless the Dauphin be in presence here,
To whom expressly I bring greeting too.

FR. KING.   For us, we will consider of this further:
To-morrow shall you bear our full intent
Back to our brother England.

84 *'long*] belong.
92 *line*] pedigree.
94 *overlook*] look over, examine.
95 *evenly*] directly.
98 *indirectly*] unjustly.
99 *challenger*] claimant.
105 *requiring*] asking.
106 *bowels*] innermost being, mercy.

DAU.   For the Dauphin,   120
     I stand here for him: what to him from England?
EXE.   Scorn and defiance; slight regard, contempt,
     And any thing that may not misbecome
     The mighty sender, doth he prize you at.
     Thus says my king; an if your father's highness
     Do not, in grant of all demands at large,
     Sweeten the bitter mock you sent his majesty,
     He'll call you to so hot an answer of it,
     That caves and womby vaultages of France
     Shall chide your trespass, and return your mock   130
     In second accent of his ordnance.
DAU.   Say, if my father render fair return,
     It is against my will; for I desire
     Nothing but odds with England: to that end,
     As matching to his youth and vanity,
     I did present him with the Paris balls.
EXE.   He'll make your Paris Louvre shake for it,
     Were it the mistress-court of mighty Europe:
     And, be assured, you'll find a difference,
     As we his subjects have in wonder found,   140
     Between the promise of his greener days
     And these he masters now: now he weighs time
     Even to the utmost grain: that you shall read
     In your own losses, if he stay in France.
FR. KING.   To-morrow shall you know our mind at full.
EXE.   Dispatch us with all speed, lest that our king
     Come here himself to question our delay;
     For he is footed in this land already.
FR. KING.   You shall be soon dispatch'd with fair conditions:
     A night is but small breath and little pause   150
     To answer matters of this consequence.
                            [Flourish. Exeunt.

---

129 *womby vaultages*] hollow places beneath the soil, the subterranean foundations.
131 *In second accent of his ordnance*] In the echo of his cannon's roar.
136 *balls*] bawdy pun and reference to tennis balls the Dauphin sent to King Henry.
137 *Louvre*] French royal palace.
148 *is footed*] has foothold.
150 *breath*] breathing space.

ACT III. — PROLOGUE

Enter Chorus

CHORUS.   Thus with imagined wing our swift scene flies
            In motion of no less celerity
            Than that of thought. Suppose that you have seen
            The well-appointed king at Hampton pier
            Embark his royalty; and his brave fleet
            With silken streamers the young Phœbus fanning:
            Play with your fancies, and in them behold
            Upon the hempen tackle ship-boys climbing;
            Hear the shrill whistle which doth order give
            To sounds confused; behold the threaden sails,   10
            Borne with the invisible and creeping wind,
            Draw the huge bottoms through the furrow'd sea,
            Breasting the lofty surge: O, do but think
            You stand upon the rivage and behold
            A city on the inconstant billows dancing;
            For so appears this fleet majestical,
            Holding due course to Harfleur. Follow, follow:
            Grapple your minds to sternage of this navy,
            And leave your England, as dead midnight still,
            Guarded with grandsires, babies and old women,   20
            Either past or not arrived to pith and puissance;
            For who is he, whose chin is but enrich'd
            With one appearing hair, that will not follow
            These cull'd and choice-drawn cavaliers to France?
            Work, work your thoughts, and therein see a siege;
            Behold the ordnance on their carriages,

1 *with imagined wing*] with the wing of imagination.
2 *celerity*] speed.
8 *hempen tackle*] the ropes that support a ship's masts.
14 *rivage*] French word for "shore."
18 *sternage*] stern, steerage; the rudder was in the stern.

34

With fatal mouths gaping on girded Harfleur.
Suppose the ambassador from the French comes back;
Tells Harry that the king doth offer him
Katharine his daughter, and with her, to dowry,   30
Some petty and unprofitable dukedoms.
The offer likes not: and the nimble gunner
With linstock now the devilish cannon touches,
                    [*Alarum, and chambers go off.*
And down goes all before them. Still be kind,
And eke out our performance with your mind.   [*Exit.*

SCENE I. *France — Before Harfleur.*

Alarum. Enter KING HENRY, EXETER, BEDFORD, GLOUCESTER,
  and Soldiers, *with scaling-ladders*

K. HEN.   Once more unto the breach, dear friends, once more;
Or close the wall up with our English dead.
In peace there's nothing so becomes a man
As modest stillness and humility:
But when the blast of war blows in our ears,
Then imitate the action of the tiger;
Stiffen the sinews, summon up the blood,
Disguise fair nature with hard-favour'd rage;
Then lend the eye a terrible aspect;
Let it pry through the portage of the head   10
Like the brass cannon; let the brow o'erwhelm it
As fearfully as doth a galled rock
O'erhang and jutty his confounded base,
Swill'd with the wild and wasteful ocean.
Now set the teeth and stretch the nostril wide,
Hold hard the breath and bend up every spirit
To his full height. On, on, you noblest English,

---

30 *to dowry*] as dowry.
32 *likes not*] pleases not.
33 *linstock*] the stick to which was attached the match for firing guns.
    chambers] small cannons.

---

 8 *hard-favour'd*] grim-faced.
 9 *terrible aspect*] terrifying appearance.
10 *portage*] portholes, eyes.
13 *jutty his confounded base*] hang over its worn-away base.
14 *Swill'd . . . ocean*] Washed over . . . by the desolating ocean.
16 *bend up*] extend.

Whose blood is fet from fathers of war-proof!
Fathers that, like so many Alexanders,
Have in these parts from morn till even fought,　　　20
And sheathed their swords for lack of argument:
Dishonour not your mothers; now attest
That those whom you call'd fathers did beget you.
Be copy now to men of grosser blood,
And teach them how to war. And you, good yeomen,
Whose limbs were made in England, show us here
The mettle of your pasture; let us swear
That you are worth your breeding; which I doubt not;
For there is none of you so mean and base,
That hath not noble lustre in your eyes.　　　30
I see you stand like greyhounds in the slips,
Straining upon the start. The game's afoot:
Follow your spirit, and upon this charge
Cry "God for Harry, England, and Saint George!"
　　　　　　　[Exeunt. Alarum, and chambers go off.

SCENE II. *The Same.*

Enter NYM, BARDOLPH, PISTOL, *and* Boy

BARD.　On, on, on, on, on! to the breach, to the breach!
NYM.　Pray thee, corporal, stay: the knocks are too hot; and, for
　　　mine own part, I have not a case of lives: the humour of it is
　　　too hot, that is the very plain-song of it.
PIST.　The plain-song is most just; for humours do abound:

　　　　　Knocks go and come; God's vassals drop and die;
　　　　　　　　And sword and shield,
　　　　　　　　In bloody field,
　　　　　　　Doth win immortal fame.

---

18 *fet*] fetched, drawn.
　war-proof] strength proved in war.
19 *Alexanders*] reference to Alexander the Great.
20 *even*] evening.
21 *argument*] opposition.
24 *copy*] models.
27 *mettle of your pasture*] quality of your breeding.
31 *slips*] leashes, which held the hounds before the game was started.

3–4 *case . . . plain-song*] A "case" is a set of four musical instruments; for the simple
　music of a "plain-song," a case would not be required.
　5 *humours*] whimsicalities, fantasies.

BOY.   Would I were in an alehouse in London! I would give all   10
my fame for a pot of ale and safety.

PIST.   And I:

> If wishes would prevail with me,
> My purpose should not fail with me,
> But thither would I hie.

BOY.   As duly, but not as truly,
                              As bird doth sing on bough.

Enter FLUELLEN

FLU.   Up to the breach, you dogs! avaunt, you cullions!
                              [*Driving them forward.*

PIST.   Be merciful, great duke, to men of mould.
Abate thy rage, abate thy manly rage,   20
Abate thy rage, great duke!
Good bawcock, bate thy rage; use lenity, sweet chuck!

NYM.   These be good humours! your honour wins bad humours.   [*Exeunt all but* Boy.

BOY.   As young as I am, I have observed these three swashers. I
am boy to them all three: but all they three, though they
would serve me, could not be man to me; for indeed three
such antics do not amount to a man. For Bardolph, he is
white-livered and red-faced; by the means whereof a' faces it
out, but fights not. For Pistol, he hath a killing tongue and a   30
quiet sword; by the means whereof a' breaks words, and
keeps whole weapons. For Nym, he hath heard that men of
few words are the best men; and therefore he scorns to say
his prayers, lest a' should be thought a coward: but his few
bad words are matched with as few good deeds; for a' never
broke any man's head but his own, and that was against a
post when he was drunk. They will steal any thing, and call
it purchase. Bardolph stole a lute-case, bore it twelve

18 *cullions*] a coarse term of abuse.
19 *great duke*] Pistol thinks to flatter Captain Fluellen by exaggerating his rank.
    men of mould] men of earth, poor mortal men.
22 *Good bawcock . . . sweet chuck*] terms of playful endearment equivalent to "my fine
    fellow" or "dear old boy."
23–24 *These be good . . . bad humours*] Nym commends Pistol's blandishments. Pistol
    conciliates bad tempers. "Your honour" means "your lordship."
25 *swashers*] swashbucklers, blusterers.
28 *antics*] buffoons.
29–30 *a' faces it out*] he puts on a brave front.
31–32 *a' breaks words, and keeps whole weapons*] he fights using words, not weapons.
38 *purchase*] a colloquial euphemism for theft.

leagues, and sold it for three half-pence. Nym and Bardolph
are sworn brothers in filching, and in Calais they stole a fire- 40
shovel: I knew by that piece of service the men would carry
coals. They would have me as familiar with men's pockets as
their gloves or their handkerchers: which makes much
against my manhood, if I should take from another's pocket
to put into mine; for it is plain pocketing up of wrongs. I
must leave them, and seek some better service: their villany
goes against my weak stomach, and therefore I must cast it
up. [*Exit.*

Re-enter FLUELLEN, GOWER *following*

GOW.   Captain Fluellen, you must come presently to the mines;
the Duke of Gloucester would speak with you. 50
FLU.   To the mines! tell you the duke, it is not so good to come
to the mines; for, look you, the mines is not according to the
disciplines of the war: the concavities of it is not sufficient;
for, look you, th' athversary, you may discuss unto the duke,
look you, is digt himself four yard under the countermines:
by Cheshu, I think a' will plow up all, if there is not better
directions.
GOW.   The Duke of Gloucester, to whom the order of the siege
is given, is altogether directed by an Irishman, a very valiant
gentleman, i' faith. 60
FLU.   It is Captain Macmorris, is it not?
GOW.   I think it be.
FLU.   By Cheshu, he is an ass, as in the world: I will verify as
much in his beard: he has no more directions in the true disciplines of the wars, look you, of the Roman disciplines, than
is a puppy-dog.

Enter MACMORRIS *and* Captain JAMY

GOW.   Here a' comes; and the Scots captain, Captain Jamy,
with him.

40 *brothers in filching*] partners in crime.
41–42 *carry coals*] perform the lowest of all domestic services — hence, submit tamely to
    humiliation.
45 *pocketing up of wrongs*] putting up with insults.
49 *the mines*] the tunnels being dug by the English under the city as part of their
    planned attack.
54–55 *th' athversary . . . the countermines*] the enemy, you must explain to the Duke, is
    digging tunnels four yards under ours.
56 *Cheshu*] Jesu, Jesus.
    plow] mispronunciation of "blow."
64 *in his beard*] to his face.

FLU.   Captain Jamy is a marvellous falorous gentleman, that is
   certain; and of great expedition and knowledge in th'   70
   aunchient wars, upon my particular knowledge of his directions: by Cheshu, he will maintain his argument as well as
   any military man in the world, in the disciplines of the pris-
   tine wars of the Romans.
JAMY.   I say gud-day, Captain Fluellen.
FLU.   God-den to your worship, good Captain James.
GOW.   How now, Captain Macmorris! have you quit the mines?
   have the pioners given o'er?
MAC.   By Chrish, la! tish ill done: the work ish give over, the
   trompet sound the retreat. By my hand, I swear, and my fa-   80
   ther's soul, the work ish ill done; it ish give over: I would
   have blowed up the town, so Chrish save me, la! in an hour:
   O, tish ill done, tish ill done; by my hand, tish ill done!
FLU.   Captain Macmorris, I beseech you now, will you voutsafe
   me, look you, a few disputations with you, as partly touching
   or concerning the disciplines of the war, the Roman wars, in
   the way of argument, look you, and friendly communica-
   tion; partly to satisfy my opinion, and partly for the satisfaction, look you, of my mind, as touching the direction of the
   military discipline; that is the point.   90
JAMY.   It sall be vary gud, gud feith, gud captains bath: and I sall
   quit you with gud leve, as I may pick occasion; that sall I,
   marry.
MAC.   It is no time to discourse, so Chrish save me: the day is
   hot, and the weather, and the wars, and the king, and the
   dukes: it is no time to discourse. The town is beseeched, and
   the trumpet call us to the breach; and we talk, and, be
   Chrish, do nothing: 't is shame for us all: so God sa' me, 't is
   shame to stand still; it is shame, by my hand: and there is
   throats to be cut, and works to be done; and there ish noth-   100
   ing done, so Chrish sa' me, la!
JAMY.   By the mess, ere theise eyes of mine take themselves to
   slomber, ay'll de gud service, or ay'll lig i' the grund for it; ay,

70 *expedition*] a combination in Fluellen's dialect of "experience" and "erudition."
76 *God-den*] a common colloquial form of "good e'en," "good evening."
78 *pioners*] pioneers, military engineers.
79 *ill*] mispronunciation of "all."
84 *voutsafe*] vouchsafe, permit.
91 *bath*] mispronunciation of "both."
92 *quit you*] requite, answer you.
102 *mess*] mass.
103 *ay 'll lig*] I'll lie.

or go to death; and ay'll pay 't as valorously as I may, that sall I suerly do, that is the breff and the long. Marry, I wad full fain hear some question 'tween you tway.

FLU. Captain Macmorris, I think, look you, under your correction, there is not many of your nation—

MAC. Of my nation! What ish my nation? Ish a villain, and a bastard, and a knave, and a rascal. What ish my nation? Who talks of my nation? 110

FLU. Look you, if you take the matter otherwise than is meant, Captain Macmorris, peradventure I shall think you do not use me with that affability as in discretion you ought to use me, look you; being as good a man as yourself, both in the disciplines of war, and in the derivation of my birth, and in other particularities.

MAC. I do not know you so good a man as myself: So Chrish save me, I will cut off your head.

GOW. Gentlemen both, you will mistake each other. 120

JAMY. A! that's a foul fault.

[*A parley sounded.*

GOW. The town sounds a parley.

FLU. Captain Macmorris, when there is more better opportunity to be required, look you, I will be so bold as to tell you I know the disciplines of war; and there is an end.

[*Exeunt.*

SCENE III. *The Same—Before the Gates.*

The Governor *and some* Citizens *on the walls; the English forces below. Enter* KING HENRY *and his train*

K. HEN. How yet resolves the governor of the town?
This is the latest parle we will admit:
Therefore to our best mercy give yourselves;
Or like to men proud of destruction
Defy us to our worst: for, as I am a soldier,
A name that in my thoughts becomes me best,

105–106 *I wad full fain hear some question*] I would very much like to hear some debate.
109 *What ish my nation?*] Macmorris sarcastically challenges Fluellen to say a word against Ireland.

---

2 *the latest parle*] i.e., "this is your last chance to surrender." Henry is warning the governor of Harfleur.

If I begin the battery once again,
I will not leave the half-achieved Harfleur
Till in her ashes she lie buried.
The gates of mercy shall be all shut up,   10
And the flesh'd soldier, rough and hard of heart,
In liberty of bloody hand shall range
With conscience wide as hell, mowing like grass
Your fresh-fair virgins and your flowering infants.
What is it then to me, if impious war,
Array'd in flames like to the prince of fiends,
Do, with his smirch'd complexion, all fell feats
Enlink'd to waste and desolation?
What is 't to me, when you yourselves are cause,
If your pure maidens fall into the hand   20
Of hot and forcing violation?
What rein can hold licentious wickedness
When down the hill he holds his fierce career?
We may as bootless spend our vain command
Upon the enraged soldiers in their spoil
As send precepts to the leviathan
To come ashore. Therefore, you men of Harfleur,
Take pity of your town and of your people,
Whiles yet my soldiers are in my command;
Whiles yet the cool and temperate wind of grace   30
O'erblows the filthy and contagious clouds
Of heady murder, spoil and villany.
If not, why, in a moment look to see
The blind and bloody soldier with foul hand
Defile the locks of your shrill-shrieking daughters;
Your fathers taken by the silver beards,
And their most reverend heads dash'd to the walls,
Your naked infants spitted upon pikes,
Whiles the mad mothers with their howls confused
Do break the clouds, as did the wives of Jewry   40
At Herod's bloody-hunting slaughtermen.
What say you? will you yield, and this avoid,

---

8 *half-achieved*] half-conquered.
11 *the flesh'd soldier*] the soldier who has first tasted blood.
18 *Enlink'd . . . desolation*] Inevitably associated with ruin and destruction.
26 *precepts*] summons.
31 *O'erblows*] Blows away, disperses.
41 *Herod's . . . slaughtermen*] Biblical reference (Matthew 2:16–18) to King Herod's
massacre of innocent children.

Or, guilty in defence, be thus destroy'd?
GOV.   Our expectation hath this day an end:
    The Dauphin, whom of succours we entreated,
    Returns us that his powers are yet not ready
    To raise so great a siege. Therefore, great king,
    We yield our town and lives to thy soft mercy.
    Enter our gates; dispose of us and ours;
    For we no longer are defensible.   50
K. HEN.   Open your gates. Come, uncle Exeter,
    Go you and enter Harfleur; there remain,
    And fortify it strongly 'gainst the French:
    Use mercy to them all. For us, dear uncle,
    The winter coming on, and sickness growing
    Upon our soldiers, we will retire to Calais.
    To-night in Harfleur will we be your guest;
    To-morrow for the march are we addrest.
        [*Flourish*. The KING *and his train enter the town*.

SCENE IV. *The French King's Palace.*

Enter KATHARINE *and* ALICE

KATH.   Alice, tu as été en Angleterre, et tu parles bien le lan-
    gage.
ALICE.   Un peu, madame.
KATH.   Je te prie, m'enseignez; il faut que j'apprenne à parler.
    Comment appelez-vous la main en Anglois?
ALICE.   La main? elle est appelée de hand.
KATH.   De hand. Et les doigts?
ALICE.   Les doigts? ma foi, j'oublie les doigts; mais je me sou-
    viendrai. Les doigts? je pense qu'ils sont appelés de fingres;
    oui, de fingres.   10
KATH.   La main, de hand; les doigts, de fingres. Je pense que je
    suis le bon écolier; j'ai gagné deux mots d'Anglois vitement.
    Comment appelez-vous les ongles?

---

43 *in defence*] i.e., by not surrendering.
45 *whom of succours*] whose help.
46 *Returns us*] Answers us.
50 *defensible*] capable of defending ourselves.
58 *addrest*] prepared.

SCENE IV] For a translation of this scene into English, see the Appendix.

ALICE.   Les ongles? nous les appelons de nails.

KATH.   De nails. Ecoutez; dites-moi, si je parle bien: de hand, de fingres, et de nails.

ALICE.   C'est bien dit, madame; il est fort bon Anglois.

KATH.   Dites-moi l'Anglois pour le bras.

ALICE.   De arm, madame.

KATH.   Et le coude?   20

ALICE.   De elbow.

KATH.   De elbow. Je m'en fais la répétition de tous les mots que vous m'avez appris dès à présent.

ALICE.   Il est trop difficile, madame, comme je pense.

KATH.   Excusez-moi, Alice; écoutez: de hand, de fingres, de nails, de arma, de bilbow.

ALICE.   De elbow, madame.

KATH.   O Seigneur Dieu, je m'en oublie! de elbow. Comment appelez-vous le col?

ALICE.   De neck, madame.   30

KATH.   De nick. Et le menton?

ALICE.   De chin.

KATH.   De sin. Le col, de nick; le menton, de sin.

ALICE.   Oui. Sauf votre honneur, en vérité, vous prononcez les mots aussi droit que les natifs d'Angleterre.

KATH.   Je ne doute point d'apprendre, par la grace de Dieu, et en peu de temps.

ALICE.   N'avez vous pas déjà oublié ce que je vous ai enseigné?

KATH.   Non, je reciterai à vous promptement: de hand, de fin-gres, de mails,—   40

ALICE.   De nails, madame.

KATH.   De nails, de arm, de ilbow.

ALICE.   Sauf votre honneur, de elbow.

KATH.   Ainsi dis-je; de elbow, de nick, et de sin. Comment ap-pelez-vous le pied et la robe?

ALICE.   De foot, madame; et de coun.

KATH.   De foot et de coun! O Seigneur Dieu! ce sont mots de son mauvais, corruptible, gros, et impudique, et non pour les dames d'honneur d'user: je ne voudrais prononcer ces mots devant les seigneurs de France pour tout le monde. Foh! le   50 foot et le coun! Néanmoins, je réciterai une autre fois ma leçon ensemble: de hand, de fingres, de nails, de arm, de elbow, de nick, de sin, de foot, de coun.

ALICE.   Excellent, madame!

KATH.   C'est assez pour une fois: allons-nous à dîner.

                                         [Exeunt.

SCENE V. *The Same.*

Enter the KING *of* FRANCE, *the* DAUPHIN, *the* DUKE *of* BOURBON,
the CONSTABLE *of* FRANCE, *and others*

FR. KING.   'T is certain he hath pass'd the river Somme.
CON.   And if he be not fought withal, my lord,
    Let us not live in France; let us quit all,
    And give our vineyards to a barbarous people.
DAU.   O Dieu vivant! shall a few sprays of us,
    The emptying of our fathers' luxury,
    Our scions, put in wild and savage stock,
    Spirt up so suddenly into the clouds,
    And overlook their grafters?
BOUR.   Normans, but bastard Normans, Norman bastards!   10
    Mort de ma vie! if they march along
    Unfought withal, but I will sell my dukedom,
    To buy a slobbery and a dirty farm
    In that nook-shotten isle of Albion.
CON.   Dieu de batailles! where have they this mettle?
    Is not their climate foggy, raw and dull,
    On whom, as in despite, the sun looks pale,
    Killing their fruit with frowns? Can sodden water,
    A drench for sur-rein'd jades, their barley-broth,
    Decoct their cold blood to such valiant heat?   20
    And shall our quick blood, spirited with wine,
    Seem frosty? O, for honour of our land,
    Let us not hang like roping icicles
    Upon our houses' thatch, whiles a more frosty people
    Sweat drops of gallant youth in our rich fields!—
    Poor we may call them in their native lords.

---

3 *quit all*] give up, yield.
5 *sprays*] sprigs or sprouts. Reference is here made to the fact that the English raiders
    are descendants of Frenchmen through William the Conqueror, who was himself
    born out of wedlock.
6 *our fathers' luxury*] our ancestors' lust.
7–9 *Our scions . . . grafters*] The image here is of the branches or scions of a tree (i.e.,
    France) being replanted in "wild and savage stock" (i.e., England) and suddenly over-
    shadowing the "tree" from which they came.
13 *slobbery*] waterlogged.
14 *nook-shotten Isle of Albion*] many-inleted island of England.
19 *A drench for sur-rein'd jades*] Liquid medicine for overworked horses.
20 *Decoct*] Boil, heat. A tonic medicine is often called a "decoction."
26 *Poor we may . . . their native lords*] We may call our *rich* fields *poor* because of the
    feeble character of their native owners.

DAU.   By faith and honour,
     Our madams mock at us, and plainly say
     Our mettle is bred out, and they will give
     Their bodies to the lust of English youth,   30
     To new-store France with bastard warriors.
BOUR.   They bid us to the English dancing-schools,
     And teach lavoltas high and swift corantos;
     Saying our grace is only in our heels,
     And that we are most lofty runaways.
FR. KING.   Where is Montjoy the herald? speed him hence:
     Let him greet England with our sharp defiance.
     Up, princes! and, with spirit of honour edged
     More sharper than your swords, hie to the field:
     Charles Delabreth, high constable of France;   40
     You Dukes of Orleans, Bourbon, and of Berri,
     Alençon, Brabant, Bar, and Burgundy;
     Jaques Chatillon, Rambures, Vaudemont,
     Beaumont, Grandpré, Roussi, and Fauconberg,
     Foix, Lestrale, Bouciqualt, and Charolois;
     High dukes, great princes, barons, lords and knights,
     For your great seats now quit you of great shames.
     Bar Harry England, that sweeps through our land
     With pennons painted in the blood of Harfleur:
     Rush on his host, as doth the melted snow   50
     Upon the valleys, whose low vassal seat
     The Alps doth spit and void his rheum upon:
     Go down upon him, you have power enough,
     And in a captive chariot into Rouen
     Bring him our prisoner.
CON.   This becomes the great.
     Sorry am I his numbers are so few,
     His soldiers sick and famish'd in their march,
     For I am sure, when he shall see our army,
     He'll drop his heart into the sink of fear   60
     And for achievement offer us his ransom.
FR. KING.   Therefore, lord constable, haste on Montjoy,
     And let him say to England that we send

33 *lavoltas and corantos*] Lively dances.
47 *For your great seats . . . you*] For (the protection of) your noble castles now acquit
    yourselves.
49 *pennons*] banners.
52 *rheum*] i.e., waters.
60 *He'll drop his heart . . . fear*] A strong expression for vomiting.
61 *for achievement*] instead of achieving victory over us, of conquering us.

To know what willing ransom he will give.
Prince Dauphin, you shall stay with us in Rouen.
DAU.   Not so, I do beseech your majesty.
FR. KING.   Be patient, for you shall remain with us.
Now forth, lord constable and princes all,
And quickly bring us word of England's fall.   [*Exeunt.*

SCENE VI. *The English Camp in Picardy.*

Enter GOWER *and* FLUELLEN, *meeting*

GOW.   How now, Captain Fluellen! come you from the bridge?
FLU.   I assure you, there is very excellent services committed at
the bridge.
GOW.   Is the Duke of Exeter safe?
FLU.   The Duke of Exeter is as magnanimous as Agamemnon;
and a man that I love and honour with my soul, and my
heart, and my duty, and my life, and my living, and my ut-
termost power: he is not—God be praised and blessed!—any
hurt in the world; but keeps the bridge most valiantly, with
excellent discipline. There is an aunchient lieutenant there   10
at the pridge, I think in my very conscience he is as valiant
a man as Mark Antony; and he is a man of no estimation in
the world; but I did see him do as gallant service.
GOW.   What do you call him?
FLU.   He is called Aunchient Pistol.
GOW.   I know him not.

Enter PISTOL

FLU.   Here is the man.
PIST.   Captain, I thee beseech to do me favours:
The Duke of Exeter doth love thee well.
FLU.   Ay, I praise God; and I have merited some love at his   20
hands.
PIST.   Bardolph, a soldier, firm and sound of heart,
And of buxom valour, hath, by cruel fate,
And giddy Fortune's furious fickle wheel,

---

1 *the bridge*] The bridge over the river Ternoise, which lay on the road of Henry's
march to Calais. The French attempt to demolish it was defeated by the English.
2 *services*] victories.
10 *aunchient lieutenant*] a confused reference to Pistol, whose rank was that of "ancient," i.e., ensign, not "lieutenant."

That goddess blind,
That stands upon the rolling restless stone—

FLU.   By your patience, Aunchient Pistol. Fortune is painted
blind, with a muffler afore her eyes, to signify to you that
Fortune is blind; and she is painted also with a wheel, to signify to you, which is the moral of it, that she is turning, and   30
inconstant, and mutability, and variation: and her foot, look
you, is fixed upon a spherical stone, which rolls, and rolls,
and rolls: in good truth, the poet makes a most excellent description of it: Fortune is an excellent moral.

PIST.   Fortune is Bardolph's foe, and frowns on him;
For he hath stolen a pax, and hanged must a' be:
A damned death!
Let gallows gape for dog; let man go free
And let not hemp his wind-pipe suffocate:
But Exeter hath given the doom of death   40
For pax of little price.
Therefore, go speak; the duke will hear thy voice;
And let not Bardolph's vital thread be cut
With edge of penny cord and vile reproach:
Speak, captain, for his life, and I will thee requite.

FLU.   Aunchient Pistol, I do partly understand your meaning.

PIST.   Why then, rejoice therefore.

FLU.   Certainly, aunchient, it is not a thing to rejoice at: for if,
look you, he were my brother, I would desire the duke to use
his good pleasure, and put him to execution; for discipline   50
ought to be used.

PIST.   Die and be damn'd! and figo for thy friendship!

FLU.   It is well.

PIST.   The fig of Spain!   [Exit.

FLU.   Very good.

GOW.   Why, this is an arrant counterfeit rascal; I remember him
now; a bawd, a cutpurse.

FLU.   I'll assure you, a' uttered as prave words at the pridge as
you shall see in a summer's day. But it is very well; what he
has spoke to me, that is well, I warrant you, when time is   60
serve.

28 *muffler*] blindfold.
36 *pax*] a small piece of plate, engraved with the picture of the crucifixion, which was
offered by the priest during Mass.
45 *requite*] repay.
52 *figo*] a fig, any contemptible trifle, a snap of the fingers.
54 *The fig of Spain*] Pistol underlines his insult by specifying the gesture made by thrust-
ing the thumb out between the first and second fingers in semblance of a vulva.

GOW. Why, 't is a gull, a fool, a rogue, that now and then goes to the wars, to grace himself at his return into London under the form of a soldier. And such fellows are perfect in the great commanders' names: and they will learn you by rote where services were done; at such and such a sconce, at such a breach, at such a convoy; who came off bravely, who was shot, who disgraced, what terms the enemy stood on; and this they con perfectly in the phrase of war, which they trick up with new-tuned oaths: and what a beard of the general's 70 cut and a horrid suit of the camp will do among foaming bottles and ale-washed wits, is wonderful to be thought on. But you must learn to know such slanders of the age, or else you may be marvellously mistook.

FLU. I tell you what, Captain Gower; I do perceive he is not the man that he would gladly make show to the world he is: if I find a hole in his coat, I will tell him my mind. [*Drum heard.*] Hark you, the king is coming, and I must speak with him from the pridge.

Drum and Colours. Enter KING HENRY, GLOUCESTER, *and* Soldiers

God pless your majesty! 80

K. HEN. How now, Fluellen! camest thou from the bridge?

FLU. Ay, so please your majesty. The Duke of Exeter has very gallantly maintained the pridge: the French is gone off, look you; and there is gallant and most prave passages: marry, th' athversary was have possession of the pridge; but he is enforced to retire, and the Duke of Exeter is master of the pridge: I can tell your majesty, the duke is a prave man.

K. HEN. What men have you lost, Fluellen?

FLU. The perdition of th' athversary hath been very great, reasonable great: marry, for my part, I think the duke hath lost 90 never a man, but one that is like to be executed for robbing a church, one Bardolph, if your majesty know the man: his face is all bubukles, and whelks, and knobs, and flames o'

---

64 *are perfect in*] i.e., can recite perfectly.
66 *sconce*] fortification.
71 *horrid suit*] war-stained uniform.
73 *slanders*] disgraces, slanderers.
78–79 *speak . . . pridge*] tell him what has happened at the bridge.
89 *perdition*] losses.
93 *bubukles*] blotches; a word made up of "buboes" and "carbuncles."
    whelks] pimples.

fire: and his lips blows at his nose, and it is like a coal of fire, sometimes plue and sometimes red; but his nose is executed, and his fire 's out.

K. HEN.   We would have all such offenders so cut off: and we give express charge, that in our marches through the country, there be nothing compelled from the villages, nothing taken but paid for, none of the French upbraided or abused   100 in disdainful language; for when lenity and cruelty play for a kingdom, the gentler gamester is the soonest winner.

Tucket. Enter MONTJOY

MONT.   You know me by my habit.

K. HEN.   Well then I know thee: what shall I know of thee?

MONT.   My master's mind.

K. HEN.   Unfold it.

MONT.   Thus says my king: Say thou to Harry of England: Though we seemed dead, we did but sleep: advantage is a better soldier than rashness. Tell him we could have rebuked him at Harfleur, but that we thought not good to bruise an   110 injury till it were full ripe: now we speak upon our cue, and our voice is imperial: England shall repent his folly, see his weakness, and admire our sufferance. Bid him therefore consider of his ransom; which must proportion the losses we have borne, the subjects we have lost, the disgrace we have digested; which in weight to re-answer, his pettiness would bow under. For our losses, his exchequer is too poor; for the effusion of our blood, the muster of his kingdom too faint a number; and for our disgrace, his own person, kneeling at our feet, but a weak and worthless satisfaction. To this add   120 defiance: and tell him, for conclusion, he hath betrayed his followers, whose condemnation is pronounced. So far my king and master; so much my office.

K. HEN.   What is thy name? I know thy quality.

MONT.   Montjoy.

---

102 *gamester*] player.
    Tucket] Flourish on a trumpet as Montjoy, the French herald, enters.
103 *habit*] The herald's coat, which was inviolable in war.
111 *upon our cue*] in our turn, at the right moment.
112 *England*] i.e., King Henry.
116 *in weight to re-answer*] to repay in full.
117 *exchequer*] treasury.
124 *quality*] rank and profession.

K. HEN.   Thou dost thy office fairly. Turn thee back,
   And tell thy king I do not seek him now;
   But could be willing to march on to Calais
   Without impeachment: for, to say the sooth,
   Though 't is no wisdom to confess so much   130
   Unto an enemy of craft and vantage,
   My people are with sickness much enfeebled,
   My numbers lessen'd, and those few I have
   Almost no better than so many French;
   Who when they were in health, I tell thee, herald,
   I thought upon one pair of English legs
   Did march three Frenchmen. Yet, forgive me, God,
   That I do brag thus! This your air of France
   Hath blown that vice in me; I must repent.
   Go therefore, tell thy master here I am;   140
   My ransom is this frail and worthless trunk,
   My army but a weak and sickly guard;
   Yet, God before, tell him we will come on,
   Though France himself and such another neighbour
   Stand in our way. There's for thy labour, Montjoy.
   Go, bid thy master well advise himself:
   If we may pass, we will; if we be hinder'd,
   We shall your tawny ground with your red blood
   Discolour: and so, Montjoy, fare you well.
   The sum of all our answer is but this: 150
   We would not seek a battle, as we are;
   Nor, as we are, we say we will not shun it:
   So tell your master.
MONT.   I shall deliver so. Thanks to your highness.   [*Exit.*
GLOU.   I hope they will not come upon us now.
K. HEN.   We are in God's hand, brother, not in theirs.
   March to the bridge; it now draws toward night:
   Beyond the river we'll encamp ourselves,
   And on to-morrow bid them march away.   [*Exeunt.*

129 *Without impeachment*] Without hindrance.
   sooth] truth.
131 *craft and vantage*] cunning and superior numbers.
141 *trunk*] body.
143 *God before*] God guiding us, with God for guide.

SCENE **VII.** *The French Camp, near Agincourt.*

Enter the CONSTABLE *of* France, *the* LORD RAMBURES, ORLEANS,
DAUPHIN, *with others*

CON.   Tut! I have the best armour of the world. Would it were
    day!

ORL.   You have an excellent armour; but let my horse have his
    due.

CON.   It is the best horse of Europe.

ORL.   Will it never be morning?

DAU.   My Lord of Orleans, and my lord high constable, you talk
    of horse and armour?

ORL.   You are as well provided of both as any prince in the
    world.   10

DAU.   What a long night is this! I will not change my horse with
    any that treads but on four pasterns. Ça, ha! he bounds from
    the earth, as if his entrails were hairs; le cheval volant, the
    Pegasus, chez les narines de feu! When I bestride him, I
    soar, I am a hawk: he trots the air; the earth sings when he
    touches it; the basest horn of his hoof is more musical than
    the pipe of Hermes.

ORL.   He's of the colour of the nutmeg.

DAU.   And of the heat of the ginger. It is a beast for Perseus: he
    is pure air and fire; and the dull elements of earth and water   20
    never appear in him, but only in patient stillness while his
    rider mounts him: he is indeed a horse; and all other jades
    you may call beasts.

CON.   Indeed, my lord, it is a most absolute and excellent horse.

DAU.   It is the prince of palfreys; his neigh is like the bidding of
    a monarch, and his countenance enforces homage.

ORL.   No more, cousin.

DAU.   Nay, the man hath no wit that cannot, from the rising of
    the lark to the lodging of the lamb, vary deserved praise on
    my palfrey: it is a theme as fluent as the sea: turn the sands   30

12 *pasterns*] i.e., hooves.
13 *as if his entrails were hairs*] a reference to the elasticity of tennis balls, which were
    stuffed with hair.
13–14 *le cheval volant . . . de feu!*] the flying horse, Pegasus, with nostrils of fire!
17 *the pipe of Hermes*] According to Ovid's *Metamorphoses*, Mercury (or Hermes) puts
    the monster Argus to sleep by the music of his pipe.
22 *jades*] a pejorative word for horses.
25 *palfreys*] saddle horses.
29 *lodging*] lying down, resting.

into eloquent tongues, and my horse is argument for them all: 't is a subject for a sovereign to reason on, and for a sovereign's sovereign to ride on; and for the world, familiar to us and unknown, to lay apart their particular functions and wonder at him. I once writ a sonnet in his praise, and began thus: "Wonder of nature," —

ORL.   I have heard a sonnet begin so to one's mistress.

DAU.   Then did they imitate that which I composed to my courser, for my horse is my mistress.

ORL.   Your mistress bears well.   40

DAU.   Me well; which is the prescript praise and perfection of a good and particular mistress.

CON.   Nay, for methought yesterday your mistress shrewdly shook your back.

DAU.   So perhaps did yours.

CON.   Mine was not bridled.

DAU.   O then belike she was old and gentle; and you rode, like a kern of Ireland, your French hose off, and in your strait strossers.

CON.   You have good judgement in horsemanship.   50

DAU.   Be warned by me, then: they that ride so, and ride not warily, fall into foul bogs. I had rather have my horse to my mistress.

CON.   I had as lief have my mistress a jade.

DAU.   I tell thee, constable, my mistress wears his own hair.

CON.   I could make as true a boast as that, if I had a sow to my mistress.

DAU.   "Le chien est retourné à son propre vomissement, et la truie lavée au bourbier:" thou makest use of any thing.

CON.   Yet do I not use my horse for my mistress, or any such   60
proverb so little kin to the purpose.

39 *my horse is my mistress*] This line begins a bawdy conversation comparing horses to mistresses. The scene emphasizes the vanity and overconfidence of the French, especially when compared to the more sober and profound sentiments on war expressed by King Henry.

41 *prescript*] prescribed, appropriate.

48–49 *a kern of Ireland . . . strossers*] An Irish kern was a lightly clad foot soldier, but here seems used in the sense of one half-naked. "French hose" were loose and wide breeches; "strait strossers" were tight breeches. The Dauphin suggests that the constable rode very lightly clad, or without wearing any clothes at all.

54 *lief*] happily.

55 *my mistress . . . hair*] a hit at the practice of wearing wigs.

58–59 *"Le chien . . . bourbier"*] A verbatim quotation from the French translation of the Bible, from 2 Peter, ii, 22, "The dog is turned to his own vomit again; and the sow that was washed to her wallowing in the mire."

RAM.   My lord constable, the armour that I saw in your tent to-
        night, are those stars or suns upon it?
CON.   Stars, my lord.
DAU.   Some of them will fall to-morrow, I hope.
CON.   And yet my sky shall not want.
DAU.   That may be, for you bear a many superfluously, and 't
        were more honour some were away.
CON.   Even as your horse bears your praises; who would trot as
        well, were some of your brags dismounted.   70
DAU.   Would I were able to load him with his desert! Will it
        never be day? I will trot to-morrow a mile, and my way shall
        be paved with English faces.
CON.   I will not say so, for fear I should be faced out of my way:
        but I would it were morning; for I would fain be about the
        ears of the English.
RAM.   Who will go to hazard with me for twenty prisoners?
CON.   You must first go yourself to hazard, ere you have them.
DAU.   'T is midnight; I'll go arm myself.   [*Exit.*
ORL.   The Dauphin longs for morning.   80
RAM.   He longs to eat the English.
CON.   I think he will eat all he kills.
ORL.   By the white hand of my lady, he's a gallant prince.
CON.   Swear by her foot, that she may tread out the oath.
ORL.   He is simply the most active gentleman of France.
CON.   Doing is activity; and he will still be doing.
ORL.   He never did harm, that I heard of.
CON.   Nor will do none to-morrow: he will keep that good name
        still.
ORL.   I know him to be valiant.   90
CON.   I was told that by one that knows him better than you.
ORL.   What's he?
CON.   Marry, he told me so himself; and he said he cared not
        who knew it.
ORL.   He needs not; it is no hidden virtue in him.
CON.   By my faith, sir, but it is; never any body saw it but his

---

74 *faced out*] bluffed out; an expression used in card games.
75–76 *fain be about the ears of*] gladly be striking the heads of.
77 *go to hazard*] gamble. (In the next line the same phrase means "put yourself in dan-
     ger.")
84 *tread out the oath*] attest the oath by dancing. This suggestion is that the prince's gal-
     lantry has more concern with dancing than with military prowess.

lackey: 't is a hooded valour; and when it appears, it will
bate.

ORL. Ill will never said well.

CON. I will cap that proverb with "There is flattery in friend- 100
ship."

ORL. And I will take up that with "Give the devil his due."

CON. Well placed: there stands your friend for the devil: have
at the very eye of that proverb with "A pox of the devil."

ORL. You are the better at proverbs, by how much "A fool's bolt
is soon shot."

CON. You have shot over.

ORL. 'T is not the first time you were overshot.

Enter a Messenger

MESS. My lord high constable, the English lie within fifteen
hundred paces of your tents. 110

CON. Who hath measured the ground?

MESS. The Lord Grandpré.

CON. A valiant and most expert gentleman. Would it were day!
Alas, poor Harry of England! he longs not for the dawning as
we do.

ORL. What a wretched and peevish fellow is this King of
England, to mope with his fat-brained followers so far out of
his knowledge!

CON. If the English had any apprehension, they would run
away. 120

ORL. That they lack; for if their heads had any intellectual armour, they could never wear such heavy head-pieces.

RAM. That island of England breeds very valiant creatures; their
mastiffs are of unmatchable courage.

ORL. Foolish curs, that run winking into the mouth of a
Russian bear and have their heads crushed like rotten

97–98 *'t is a hooded valour . . . bate*] The language belongs to the sport of falconry. The
falcon's head was covered with a hood until the falconer wanted it to fly. To "bate"
is to flutter the wings (instead of going after prey). The constable suggests that the
Dauphin's valor is all talk and bluster.

105 *bolt*] short, blunt arrow.

107 *shot over*] missed the mark.

108 *overshot*] The word had two meanings: "put to shame" and "intoxicated" or
"drunk."

119 *apprehension*] sense, intelligence.

124 *mastiffs*] a breed of large dogs.

125 *winking*] with their eyes closed.

apples! You may as well say, that's a valiant flea that dare eat
his breakfast on the lip of a lion.

CON.   Just, just; and the men do sympathize with the mastiffs in
robustious and rough coming on, leaving their wits with   130
their wives: and then give them great meals of beef, and iron
and steel, they will eat like wolves, and fight like devils.

ORL.   Ay, but these English are shrewdly out of beef.

CON.   Then shall we find to-morrow they have only stomachs to
eat and none to fight. Now is it time to arm: come, shall we
about it?

ORL.   It is now two o'clock: but, let me see, by ten
We shall have each a hundred Englishmen.   [*Exeunt.*

---

130 *robustious*] boisterous.

ACT IV. — PROLOGUE

Enter Chorus

CHORUS.　Now entertain conjecture of a time
　　　When creeping murmur and the poring dark
　　　Fills the wide vessel of the universe.
　　　From camp to camp through the foul womb of night
　　　The hum of either army stilly sounds,
　　　That the fix'd sentinels almost receive
　　　The secret whispers of each other's watch:
　　　Fire answers fire, and through their paly flames
　　　Each battle sees the other's umber'd face;
　　　Steed threatens steed, in high and boastful neighs　　10
　　　Piercing the night's dull ear; and from the tents
　　　The armourers, accomplishing the knights,
　　　With busy hammers closing rivets up,
　　　Give dreadful note of preparation:
　　　The country cocks do crow, the clocks do toll,
　　　And the third hour of drowsy morning name.
　　　Proud of their numbers and secure in soul,
　　　The confident and over-lusty French
　　　Do the low-rated English play at dice;
　　　And chide the cripple tardy-gaited night　　20
　　　Who, like a foul and ugly witch, doth limp
　　　So tediously away. The poor condemned English,
　　　Like sacrifices, by their watchful fires
　　　Sit patiently and inly ruminate
　　　The morning's danger, and their gesture sad
　　　Investing lank-lean cheeks and war-worn coats

2 *poring*] in which one must strain to see.
9 *umber'd*] shadowed.
12 *accomplishing*] equipping.
17 *secure in soul*] overconfident.
25–26 *their gesture sad . . . coats*] the sadness of their gesture, which communicates it-
　　self to their lank-lean cheeks and to their ragged coats.

56

Presenteth them unto the gazing moon
So many horrid ghosts. O now, who will behold
The royal captain of this ruin'd band
Walking from watch to watch, from tent to tent,   30
Let him cry "Praise and glory on his head!"
For forth he goes and visits all his host,
Bids them good morrow with a modest smile,
And calls them brothers, friends and countrymen.
Upon his royal face there is no note
How dread an army hath enrounded him;
Nor doth he dedicate one jot of colour
Unto the weary and all-watched night,
But freshly looks and over-bears attaint
With cheerful semblance and sweet majesty;   40
That every wretch, pining and pale before,
Beholding him, plucks comfort from his looks:
A largess universal like the sun
His liberal eye doth give to every one,
Thawing cold fear, that mean and gentle all
Behold, as may unworthiness define,
A little touch of Harry in the night.
And so our scene must to the battle fly;
Where—O for pity!—we shall much disgrace
With four or five most vile and ragged foils,   50
Right ill-disposed in brawl ridiculous,
The name of Agincourt. Yet sit and see,
Minding true things by what their mockeries be.   [*Exit.*

SCENE I. *The English Camp at Agincourt.*

Enter KING HENRY, BEDFORD, *and* GLOUCESTER

K. HEN.   Gloucester, 't is true that we are in great danger;
      The greater therefore should our courage be.
      Good morrow, brother Bedford. God Almighty!
      There is some soul of goodness in things evil,

---

36 *enrounded*] surrounded.
39 *over-bears attaint*] overcomes the effects of fatigue.
46 *as may unworthiness define*] i.e., as we can describe to you only imperfectly.
53 *mockeries*] inadequate imitations.

Would men observingly distil it out.
For our bad neighbour makes us early stirrers,
Which is both healthful and good husbandry:
Besides, they are our outward consciences,
And preachers to us all, admonishing
That we should dress us fairly for our end.   10
Thus may we gather honey from the weed,
And make a moral of the devil himself.

Enter ERPINGHAM

Good morrow, old Sir Thomas Erpingham:
A good soft pillow for that good white head
Were better than a churlish turf of France.
ERP.   Not so, my liege: this lodging likes me better,
Since I may say "Now lie I like a king."
K. HEN.   'T is good for men to love their present pains
Upon example; so the spirit is eased:
And when the mind is quicken'd, out of doubt,   20
The organs, though defunct and dead before,
Break up their drowsy grave and newly move,
With casted slough and fresh legerity.
Lend me thy cloak, Sir Thomas. Brothers both,
Commend me to the princes in our camp;
Do my good morrow to them, and anon
Desire them all to my pavilion.
GLOU.   We shall, my liege.
ERP.   Shall I attend your grace?
K. HEN.   No, my good knight;   30
Go with my brothers to my lords of England:
I and my bosom must debate a while,
And then I would no other company.
ERP.   The Lord in heaven bless thee, noble Harry!

                        [*Exeunt all but* KING.

K. HEN.   God-a-mercy, old heart! thou speak'st cheerfully.

Enter PISTOL

PIST.   Qui va là?

5 *observingly*] observantly.
7 *husbandry*] economy, thrift.
10 *dress us*] address, prepare ourselves.
15 *churlish*] rough, hard.
23 *casted slough*] as though having shed old skin, like a snake.
    legerity] nimbleness.
36 *Qui va là?*] Who goes there?

K. HEN.   A friend.
PIST.   Discuss unto me; art thou officer?
  Or art thou base, common, and popular?
K. HEN.   I am a gentleman of a company.   40
PIST.   Trail'st thou the puissant pike?
K. HEN.   Even so. What are you?
PIST.   As good a gentleman as the emperor.
K. HEN.   Then you are a better than the king.
PIST.   The king's a bawcock, and a heart of gold,
    A lad of life, an imp of fame;
    Of parents good, of fist most valiant:
    I kiss his dirty shoe, and from heart-string
    I love the lovely bully. What is thy name?
K. HEN.   Harry le Roy.   50
PIST.   Le Roy! a Cornish name: art thou of Cornish crew?
K. HEN.   No, I am a Welshman.
PIST.   Know'st thou Fluellen?
K. HEN.   Yes.
PIST.   Tell him, I'll knock his leek about his pate
    Upon Saint Davy's day.
K. HEN.   Do not you wear your dagger in your cap that day, lest
  he knock that about yours.
PIST.   Art thou his friend?
K. HEN.   And his kinsman too.   60
PIST.   The figo for thee, then!
K. HEN.   I thank you: God be with you!
PIST.   My name is Pistol call'd.   [*Exit.*
K. HEN.   It sorts well with your fierceness.

Enter FLUELLEN *and* GOWER

GOW.   Captain Fluellen!
FLU.   So! in the name of Jesu Christ, speak lower. It is the greatest admiration in the universal world, when the true and
  aunchient prerogatifes and laws of the wars is not kept: if you
  would take the pains but to examine the wars of Pompey the
  Great, you shall find, I warrant you, that there is no tiddle   70

41 *Trail'st . . . pike?*] i.e., are you in the infantry?
45 *bawcock*] a good fellow.
46 *imp*] scion, sprout.
49 *bully*] fine chap.
55 *leek*] a plant worn by Welshmen to commemorate a victory over the Saxons.
  pate] head.
61 *figo*] insulting gesture. (See above, III, vi, 54.)
68 *aunchient prerogatifes*] old rules.

taddle nor pibble pabble in Pompey's camp; I warrant you, you shall find the ceremonies of the wars, and the cares of it, and the forms of it, and the sobriety of it, and the modesty of it, to be otherwise.

GOW.   Why, the enemy is loud; you hear him all night.

FLU.   If the enemy is an ass and a fool and a prating coxcomb, is it meet, think you, that we should also, look you, be an ass and a fool and a prating coxcomb? in your own conscience, now?

GOW.   I will speak lower.   80

FLU.   I pray you and beseech you that you will.

                   [*Exeunt* GOWER *and* FLUELLEN.

K. HEN.   Though it appear a little out of fashion,
There is much care and valour in this Welshman.

Enter three soldiers, JOHN BATES, ALEXANDER COURT, *and*
MICHAEL WILLIAMS

COURT.   Brother John Bates, is not that the morning which breaks yonder?

BATES.   I think it be: but we have no great cause to desire the approach of day.

WILL.   We see yonder the beginning of the day, but I think we shall never see the end of it. Who goes there?

K. HEN.   A friend.   90

WILL.   Under what captain serve you?

K. HEN.   Under Sir Thomas Erpingham.

WILL.   A good old commander and a most kind gentleman: I pray you, what thinks he of our estate?

K. HEN.   Even as men wrecked upon a sand, that look to be washed off the next tide.

BATES.   He hath not told his thought to the king?

K. HEN.   No; nor it is not meet he should. For, though I speak it to you, I think the king is but a man, as I am: the violet smells to him as it doth to me; the element shows to him as   100
it doth to me; all his senses have but human conditions: his ceremonies laid by, in his nakedness he appears but a man; and though his affections are higher mounted than ours, yet,

76 *prating coxcomb*] loud, chattering fool.
94 *our estate*] our situation.
95 *wrecked*] shipwrecked.
100 *the element*] the sky.
103 *are higher mounted*] soar higher.

when they stoop, they stoop with the like wing. Therefore
when he sees reason of fears, as we do, his fears, out of
doubt, be of the same relish as ours are: yet, in reason, no
man should possess him with any appearance of fear, lest he,
by showing it, should dishearten his army.

BATES.   He may show what outward courage he will; but I believe, as cold a night as 't is, he could wish himself in   110
Thames up to the neck; and so I would he were, and I by
him, at all adventures, so we were quit here.

K. HEN.   By my troth, I will speak my conscience of the king: I
think he would not wish himself any where but where he is.

BATES.   Then I would he were here alone; so should he be sure
to be ransomed, and a many poor men's lives saved.

K. HEN.   I dare say you love him not so ill, to wish him here
alone, howsoever you speak this to feel other men's minds:
methinks I could not die any where so contented as in the
king's company; his cause being just and his quarrel hon-   120
ourable.

WILL.   That's more than we know.

BATES.   Ay, or more than we should seek after; for we know
enough, if we know we are the king's subjects: if his cause be
wrong, our obedience to the king wipes the crime of it out
of us.

WILL.   But if the cause be not good, the king himself hath a
heavy reckoning to make, when all those legs and arms and
heads, chopped off in a battle, shall join together at the latter day and cry all "We died at such a place"; some swearing,   130
some crying for a surgeon, some upon their wives left poor
behind them, some upon the debts they owe, some upon
their children rawly left. I am afeard there are few die well
that die in a battle; for how can they charitably dispose of any
thing, when blood is their argument? Now, if these men do
not die well, it will be a black matter for the king that led
them to it; whom to disobey were against all proportion of
subjection.

K. HEN.   So, if a son that is by his father sent about merchandise

---

112 *at all adventures*] no matter what happens.
   quit here] gone from here.
129–130 *at the latter day*] at the last day, at the day of judgment.
133 *rawly left*] left young and helpless.
135 *when blood . . . argument*] when shedding of blood is the subject of their thought,
   their business in hand.
137–138 *proportion of subjection*] proper duty of a subject.

do sinfully miscarry upon the sea, the imputation of his   140
wickedness, by your rule, should be imposed upon his father
that sent him: or if a servant, under his master's command
transporting a sum of money, be assailed by robbers and die
in many irreconciled iniquities, you may call the business of
the master the author of the servant's damnation: but this is
not so: the king is not bound to answer the particular end-
ings of his soldiers, the father of his son, nor the master of his
servant; for they purpose not their death, when they purpose
their services. Besides, there is no king, be his cause never so
spotless, if it come to the arbitrement of swords, can try it out   150
with all unspotted soldiers: some peradventure have on them
the guilt of premeditated and contrived murder; some, of be-
guiling virgins with the broken seals of perjury; some, making the wars their bulwark, that have before gored the gentle
bosom of peace with pillage and robbery. Now, if these men
have defeated the law and outrun native punishment,
though they can outstrip men, they have no wings to fly from
God: war is His beadle, war is His vengeance; so that here
men are punished for before-breach of the king's laws in now
the king's quarrel: where they feared the death, they have   160
borne life away; and where they would be safe, they perish:
then if they die unprovided, no more is the king guilty of
their damnation than he was before guilty of those impieties
for the which they are now visited. Every subject's duty is the
king's; but every subject's soul is his own. Therefore should
every soldier in the wars do as every sick man in his bed,
wash every mote out of his conscience: and dying so, death
is to him advantage; or not dying, the time was blessedly lost
wherein such preparation was gained: and in him that es-
capes, it were not sin to think that, making God so free an   170
offer, He let him outlive that day to see His greatness and to
teach others how they should prepare.

140 *sinfully miscarry*] perish in sin; die without repenting their sins.
148 *purpose*] intend.
150 *arbitrement*] arbitration, settling of a dispute.
151 *peradventure*] perhaps.
152 *contrived*] actually committed.
156 *native*] at home.
158 *beadle*] parish officer who punishes petty offenders.
162 *unprovided*] unprepared spiritually.
167 *mote*] small impurity.

WILL.   'T is certain, every man that dies ill, the ill upon his own head, the king is not to answer it.

BATES.   I do not desire he should answer for me; and yet I determine to fight lustily for him.

K. HEN.   I myself heard the king say he would not be ransomed.

WILL.   Ay, he said so, to make us fight cheerfully: but when our throats are cut, he may be ransomed, and we ne'er the wiser.

K. HEN.   If I live to see it, I will never trust his word after.   180

WILL.   You pay him then. That's a perilous shot out of an elder-gun, that a poor and a private displeasure can do against a monarch! you may as well go about to turn the sun to ice with fanning in his face with a peacock's feather. You'll never trust his word after! come, 't is a foolish saying.

K. HEN.   Your reproof is something too round: I should be angry with you, if the time were convenient.

WILL.   Let it be a quarrel between us, if you live.

K. HEN.   I embrace it.

WILL.   How shall I know thee again?   190

K. HEN.   Give me any gage of thine, and I will wear it in my bonnet: then, if ever thou darest acknowledge it, I will make it my quarrel.

WILL.   Here's my glove: give me another of thine.

K. HEN.   There.

WILL.   This will I also wear in my cap: if ever thou come to me and say, after to-morrow, "This is my glove," by this hand, I will take thee a box on the ear.

K. HEN.   If ever I live to see it, I will challenge it.

WILL.   Thou darest as well be hanged.   200

K. HEN.   Well, I will do it, though I take thee in the king's company.

WILL.   Keep thy word: fare thee well.

BATES.   Be friends, you English fools, be friends: we have French quarrels enow, if you could tell how to reckon.

K. HEN.   Indeed, the French may lay twenty French crowns to one, they will beat us; for they bear them on their shoulders:

---

173 *dies ill*] dies in sin.
181–182 *an elder-gun*] a toy gun made of elder word.
186 *round*] blunt, outspoken.
191 *gage*] pledge.
192 *bonnet*] military headgear.
198 *take*] give, strike.

but it is no English treason to cut French crowns, and to-
morrow the king himself will be a clipper.

                                       [*Exeunt* Soldiers.

Upon the king! let us our lives, our souls,   210
Our debts, our careful wives,
Our children and our sins lay on the king!
We must bear all. O hard condition,
Twin-born with greatness, subject to the breath
Of every fool, whose sense no more can feel
But his own wringing! What infinite heart's-ease
Must kings neglect, that private men enjoy!
And what have kings, that privates have not too,
Save ceremony, save general ceremony?
And what art thou, thou idol ceremony?   220
What kind of god art thou, that suffer'st more
Of mortal griefs than do thy worshippers?
What are thy rents? what are thy comings in?
O ceremony, show me but thy worth!
What is thy soul of adoration?
Art thou aught else but place, degree and form,
Creating awe and fear in other men?
Wherein thou art less happy being fear'd
Than they in fearing.
What drink'st thou oft, instead of homage sweet,   230
But poison'd flattery? O, be sick, great greatness,
And bid thy ceremony give thee cure!
Think'st thou the fiery fever will go out
With titles blown from adulation?
Will it give place to flexure and low bending?
Canst thou, when thou command'st the beggar's knee,
Command the health of it? No, thou proud dream,
That play'st so subtly with a king's repose;
I am a king that find thee, and I know
'T is not the balm, the sceptre and the ball,   240

208 *cut French crowns*] an allusion to the felonious practice of cutting pieces off coins,
    with a pun on crowns in the sense of heads.
211 *careful*] anxious.
215–216 *whose sense . . . wringing*] who has no feeling for any suffering save that which
    wrings his own heart, that which he endures himself.
225 *thy soul of adoration*] the essential virtue which men adore in thee.
234 *blown from adulation*] blown from the lips of flatterers.
235 *flexure*] bending.
238 *repose*] rest, sleep.
239 *balm*] oil used at the king's coronation.

The sword, the mace, the crown imperial,
The intertissued robe of gold and pearl,
The farced title running 'fore the king,
The throne he sits on, nor the tide of pomp
That beats upon the high shore of this world,
No, not all these, thrice-gorgeous ceremony,
Not all these, laid in bed majestical,
Can sleep so soundly as the wretched slave,
Who with a body fill'd and vacant mind
Gets him to rest, cramm'd with distressful bread;   250
Never sees horrid night, the child of hell,
But, like a lackey, from the rise to set
Sweats in the eye of Phœbus and all night
Sleeps in Elysium; next day after dawn,
Doth rise and help Hyperion to his horse,
And follows so the ever-running year,
With profitable labour, to his grave:
And, but for ceremony, such a wretch,
Winding up days with toil and nights with sleep,
Had the fore-hand and vantage of a king.   260
The slave, a member of the country's peace,
Enjoys it; but in gross brain little wots
What watch the king keeps to maintain the peace,
Whose hours the peasant best advantages.

Re-enter ERPINGHAM

ERP.   My lord, your nobles, jealous of your absence,
    Seek through your camp to find you.
K. HEN.   Good old knight,
    Collect them all together at my tent:
    I'll be before thee.
ERP.   I shall do't, my lord.   [*Exit.*   270
K. HEN.   O God of battles! steel my soldiers' hearts;
    Possess them not with fear; take from them now

243 *farced*] swollen, pompous.
250 *distressful*] earned by the pain of hard work.
252 *a lackey*] constant attendant, servant.
253 *Phœbus*] the sun god.
254 *Elysium*] in Greek mythology, resting place for the blessed.
255 *Hyperion*] the charioteer who pulls the sun across the sky.
260 *fore-hand and vantage*] upper hand and advantage.
262 *wots*] knows.
264 *best advantages*] applies to best advantage.
265 *jealous of*] anxious about.

The sense of reckoning, if the opposed numbers
Pluck their hearts from them. Not to-day, O Lord,
O, not to-day, think not upon the fault
My father made in compassing the crown!
I Richard's body have interred new;
And on it have bestow'd more contrite tears
Than from it issued forced drops of blood:
Five hundred poor I have in yearly pay, 280
Who twice a-day their wither'd hands hold up
Toward heaven, to pardon blood; and I have built
Two chantries, where the sad and solemn priests
Sing still for Richard's soul. More will I do;
Though all that I can do is nothing worth,
Since that my penitence comes after all,
Imploring pardon.

Re-enter GLOUCESTER

GLOU.   My liege!
K. HEN.   My brother Gloucester's voice? Ay;
    I know thy errand, I will go with thee: 290
    The day, my friends and all things stay for me.   [*Exeunt.*

SCENE II. *The French Camp.*

Enter DAUPHIN, ORLEANS, RAMBURES, *and others*

ORL.   The sun doth gild our armour; up, my lords!
DAU.   Montez à cheval! My horse! varlet! laquais! ha!
ORL.   O brave spirit!
DAU.   Via! les eaux et la terre.
ORL.   Rien puis? l'air et le feu.
DAU.   Ciel, cousin Orleans.

Enter CONSTABLE

    Now, my lord constable!

273–274 *The sense of . . . hearts from them*] their ability to count, if the enemy are so
    many as to make them fearful.
275–276 *the fault . . . the crown*] reference to the murder of King Richard II.
283 *chantries*] chapels in which masses for the dead are held.

---

2 *Montez . . . laquais!*] Mount your horses! My horse! page! footman!
4 *Via! . . . terre.*] Away with water and earth! (See above, III, vii, 20.)
5 *Rien . . . feu.*] Nothing left but air and fire?
6 *Ciel*] Sky, heaven.

CON.   Hark, how our steeds for present service neigh!
DAU.   Mount them, and make incision in their hides,
     That their hot blood may spin in English eyes,   10
     And dout them with superfluous courage, ha!
RAM.   What, will you have them weep our horses' blood?
     How shall we then behold their natural tears?

Enter MESSENGER

MESS.   The English are embattled, you French peers.
CON.   To horse, you gallant princes! straight to horse!
     Do but behold yon poor and starved band,
     And your fair show shall suck away their souls,
     Leaving them but the shales and husks of men.
     There is not work enough for all our hands;
     Scarce blood enough in all their sickly veins   20
     To give each naked curtle-axe a stain,
     That our French gallants shall to-day draw out,
     And sheathe for lack of sport: let us but blow on them,
     The vapour of our valour will o'erturn them.
     'T is positive 'gainst all exceptions, lords,
     That our superfluous lackeys and our peasants,
     Who in unnecessary action swarm
     About our squares of battle, were enow
     To purge this field of such a hilding foe,
     Though we upon this mountain's basis by   30
     Took stand for idle speculation:
     But that our honours must not. What's to say?
     A very little little let us do,
     And all is done. Then let the trumpets sound
     The tucket sonance and the note to mount;
     For our approach shall so much dare the field
     That England shall couch down in fear and yield.

   9 *incision*] i.e., with spurs.
  11 *dout*] put out
  16 *poor and starved band*] the English army, which is low on provisions and vastly out-
     numbered by the French.
  18 *shales*] shells or pods.
  21 *curtle-axe*] broad, curving sword.
  29 *hilding*] worthless, base.
  31 *Took . . . speculation*] Merely stood idly looking on.
  35 *The tucket sonance*] The trumpet blast.
  36 *dare the field*] a term in falconry, used of the hawk when, rising in the air, it terrifies
     birds on the ground. The French believe the very size of their forces will scare the
     English into retreat.

Enter GRANDPRÉ

GRAND.　Why do you stay so long, my lords of France?
　　　Yon island carrions, desperate of their bones,
　　　Ill-favouredly become the morning field:　　　　　　40
　　　Their ragged curtains poorly are let loose,
　　　And our air shakes them passing scornfully:
　　　Big Mars seems bankrupt in their beggar'd host
　　　And faintly through a rusty beaver peeps:
　　　The horsemen sit like fixed candlesticks,
　　　With torch-staves in their hand; and their poor jades
　　　Lob down their heads, dropping the hides and hips,
　　　The gum down-roping from their pale-dead eyes,
　　　And in their pale dull mouths the gimmal bit
　　　Lies foul with chew'd grass, still and motionless;　　50
　　　And their executors, the knavish crows,
　　　Fly o'er them, all impatient for their hour.
　　　Description cannot suit itself in words
　　　To demonstrate the life of such a battle
　　　In life so lifeless as it shows itself.
CON.　They have said their prayers, and they stay for death.
DAU.　Shall we go send them dinners and fresh suits
　　　And give their fasting horses provender,
　　　And after fight with them?
CON.　I stay but for my guidon: to the field!　　　　　　60
　　　I will the banner from a trumpet take,
　　　And use it for my haste. Come, come, away!
　　　The sun is high, and we outwear the day.　　　[*Exeunt.*

40 *Ill-favouredly become the . . . field*] Make a poor show on the field.
41 *curtains*] flags, pennats.
43 *Mars*] god of war.
44 *beaver*] face-guard of the helmet.
48 *down-roping*] hanging down in rope-like fashion.
49 *gimmal bit*] bit formed of a chain or interlinked rings.
51 *the knavish crows*] the birds of prey, circling overhead.
52 *their hour*] their hour of death.
54 *a battle*] the English army.
60 *guidon*] standard or ensign.
61 *the banner from a trumpet*] the banner or small flag held by the trumpeter.

SCENE III. *The English Camp.*

Enter GLOUCESTER, BEDFORD, EXETER, ERPINGHAM, *with all his*
   host: SALISBURY *and* WESTMORELAND

GLOU.   Where is the king?
BED.   The king himself is rode to view their battle.
WEST.   Of fighting men they have full three score thousand.
EXE.   There's five to one; besides, they all are fresh.
SAL.   God's arm strike with us! 't is a fearful odds.
   God be wi' you, princes all; I'll to my charge:
   If we no more meet till we meet in heaven,
   Then, joyfully, my noble Lord of Bedford,
   My dear Lord Gloucester, and my good Lord Exeter,
   And my kind kinsman, warriors all, adieu!   10
BED.   Farewell, good Salisbury; and good luck go with thee!
EXE.   Farewell, kind lord; fight valiantly to-day:
   And yet I do thee wrong to mind thee of it,
   For thou art framed of the firm truth of valour.

                                            [*Exit* SALISBURY.

BED.   He is as full of valour as of kindness;
   Princely in both.

Enter the KING

WEST.   O that we now had here
   But one ten thousand of those men in England
   That do no work to-day!
K. HEN.   What's he that wishes so?   20
   My cousin Westmoreland? No, my fair cousin:
   If we are mark'd to die, we are enow
   To do our country loss; and if to live,
   The fewer men, the greater share of honour.
   God's will! I pray thee, wish not one man more.
   By Jove, I am not covetous for gold,
   Nor care I who doth feed upon my cost;
   It yearns me not if men my garments wear;
   Such outward things dwell not in my desires:

   4 *five to one*] the amount by which the French force is estimated to outnumber the
   English.
   20 *What's he*] Who is he.
   22 *enow*] enough.
   27 *upon my cost*] at my expense.
   28 *yearns*] grieves.

But if it be a sin to covet honour,   30
I am the most offending soul alive.
No, faith, my coz, wish not a man from England:
God's peace! I would not lose so great an honour
As one man more, methinks, would share from me
For the best hope I have. O, do not wish one more!
Rather proclaim it, Westmoreland, through my host,
That he which hath no stomach to this fight,
Let him depart; his passport shall be made
And crowns for convoy put into his purse:
We would not die in that man's company   40
That fears his fellowship to die with us.
This day is call'd the feast of Crispian:
He that outlives this day, and comes safe home,
Will stand a tip-toe when this day is named,
And rouse him at the name of Crispian.
He that shall live this day, and see old age,
Will yearly on the vigil feast his neighbours,
And say, "To-morrow is Saint Crispian":
Then will he strip his sleeve and show his scars,
And say "These wounds I had on Crispin's day."   50
Old men forget; yet all shall be forgot,
But he'll remember with advantages
What feats he did that day: then shall our names,
Familiar in his mouth as household words,
Harry the king, Bedford and Exeter,
Warwick and Talbot, Salisbury and Gloucester,
Be in their flowing cups freshly remember'd.
This story shall the good man teach his son;
And Crispin Crispian shall ne'er go by,
From this day to the ending of the world,   60
But we in it shall be remembered;
We few, we happy few, we band of brothers;
For he to-day that sheds his blood with me
Shall be my brother; be he ne'er so vile,
This day shall gentle his condition:

32 *coz*] cousin.
41 *That fears . . . with us*] That fears to be our comrade in death.
42 *the feast of Crispian*] October 25 was the day of two brothers, Crispin and Crispian,
    who suffered martyrdom for their fidelity to Christianity at Soissons, about 300 A.D.
47 *the vigil*] the eve of the festival.
52 *with advantages*] with embellishments.
64 *vile*] lowly.
65 *gentle his condition*] raise him to rank of gentleman.

And gentlemen in England now a-bed
Shall think themselves accursed they were not here,
And hold their manhoods cheap whiles any speaks
That fought with us upon Saint Crispin's day.

Re-enter SALISBURY

SAL.   My sovereign lord, bestow yourself with speed: 70
     The French are bravely in their battles set,
     And will with all expedience charge on us.
K. HEN.   All things are ready, if our minds be so.
WEST.   Perish the man whose mind is backward now!
K. HEN.   Thou dost not wish more help from England, coz?
WEST.   God's will! my liege, would you and I alone,
     Without more help, could fight this royal battle!
K. HEN.   Why, now thou hast unwish'd five thousand men;
     Which likes me better than to wish us one.
     You know your places: God be with you all!   80

Tucket. Enter MONTJOY

MONT.   Once more I come to know of thee, King Harry,
     If for thy ransom thou wilt now compound,
     Before thy most assured overthrow:
     For certainly thou art so near the gulf,
     Thou needs must be englutted. Besides, in mercy,
     The constable desires thee thou wilt mind
     Thy followers of repentance; that their souls
     May make a peaceful and a sweet retire
     From off these fields, where, wretches, their poor bodies
     Must lie and fester.   90
K. HEN.   Who hath sent thee now?
MONT.   The Constable of France.
K. HEN.   I pray thee, bear my former answer back:
     Bid them achieve me and then sell my bones.
     Good God! why should they mock poor fellows thus?
     The man that once did sell the lion's skin

70 *bestow yourself*] prepare battle positions.
71 *in their battles set*] lined up in their battalions.
72 *expedience*] speed.
74 *backward*] hesitant, afraid.
84 *gulf*] whirlpool.
85 *englutted*] engulfed, swallowed up.
86 *thou wilt mind*] that you will remind.
88 *retire*] retreat, withdrawal.
94 *achieve*] conquer, finish off.

While the beast lived, was killed with hunting him.
A many of our bodies shall no doubt
Find native graves; upon the which, I trust,
Shall witness live in brass of this day's work: 100
And those that leave their valiant bones in France,
Dying like men, though buried in your dunghills,
They shall be famed; for there the sun shall greet them,
And draw their honours reeking up to heaven;
Leaving their earthly parts to choke your clime,
The smell whereof shall breed a plague in France.
Mark then abounding valour in our English,
That being dead, like to the bullet's grazing,
Break out into a second course of mischief,
Killing in relapse of mortality.   110
Let me speak proudly: tell the constable
We are but warriors for the working-day;
Our gayness and our gilt are all besmirch'd
With rainy marching in the painful field;
There's not a piece of feather in our host—
Good argument, I hope, we will not fly—
And time hath worn us into slovenry:
But, by the mass, our hearts are in the trim;
And my poor soldiers tell me, yet ere night
They'll be in fresher robes, or they will pluck   120
The gay new coats o'er the French soldiers' heads
And turn them out of service. If they do this,—
As, if God please, they shall,—my ransom then
Will soon be levied. Herald, save thou thy labour;
Come thou no more for ransom, gentle herald:
They shall have none, I swear, but these my joints;
Which if they have as I will leave 'em them,
Shall yield them little, tell the constable.
MONT.   I shall, King Harry. And so fare thee well:
Thou never shalt hear herald any more.   [*Exit.*   130
K. HEN.   I fear thou'lt once more come again for ransom.

Enter YORK

107 *abounding*] abundant.
108 *the bullet's grazing*] the bullet's ricocheting after grazing.
110 *Killing . . . mortality*] Killing when they are at the point of death.
113 *gilt*] gilding, outward brilliance.
116 *slovenry*] appearing unclean.
118 *in the trim*] prepared.

YORK.   My lord, most humbly on my knee I beg
    The leading of the vaward.
K. HEN.   Take it, brave York. Now, soldiers, march away:
    And how thou pleasest, God, dispose the day!   [*Exeunt.*

SCENE IV. *The Field of Battle.*

Alarum. Excursions. Enter PISTOL, French Soldier, *and* Boy

PIST.   Yield, cur!
FR. SOL.   Je pense que vous êtes gentilhomme de bonne qualité.
PIST.   Qualtitie calmie custure me! Art thou a gentleman? what
    is thy name? discuss.
FR. SOL.   O Seigneur Dieu!
PIST.   O, Signieur Dew should be a gentleman:
    Perpend my words, O Signieur Dew, and mark;
    O Signieur Dew, thou diest on point of fox,
    Except, O signieur, thou do give to me
    Egregious ransom.   10
FR. SOL.   O, prenez miséricorde! ayez pitié de moi!
PIST.   Moy shall not serve; I will have forty moys;
    Or I will fetch thy rim out at thy throat
    In drops of crimson blood.
FR. SOL.   Est-il impossible d'échapper la force de ton bras?
PIST.   Brass, cur!
    Thou damned and luxurious mountain goat,
    Offer'st me brass?

---

133 *vaward*] vanguard.

---

2 *Je . . . qualité.*] I think that you're a gentleman of noble lineage.
3 *calmie custure me*] This gibberish seems suggested by a favorite Irish air of the day,
    called "Calen o custure me," meaning "I am a girl from beside the [river] Suir."
5 *O . . . Dieu!*] O Lord God!
7 *Perpend*] Consider.
8 *fox*] sword.
10 *Egregious*] Enormous.
11 *O, prenez . . . moi!*] O, have mercy! take pity on me!
12 *Moy*] a bushel of corn.
13 *rim*] rim, or membrane, of the belly.
15 *Est-il . . . bras?*] Is it impossible to escape the strength of your arm?
17 *luxurious*] lascivious.

FR. SOL.   O pardonnez moi!

PIST.   Say'st thou me so? is that a ton of moys?   20
     Come hither, boy: ask me this slave in French
     What is his name.

BOY.   Écoutez: comment êtes-vous appelé?

FR. SOL.   Monsieur le Fer.

BOY.   He says his name is Master Fer.

PIST.   Master Fer! I'll fer him, and firk him, and ferret him: discuss the same in French unto him.

BOY.   I do not know the French for fer, and ferret, and firk.

PIST.   Bid him prepare; for I will cut his throat.

FR. SOL.   Que dit-il, monsieur?   30

BOY.   Il me commande de vous dire que vous faites vous prêt;
car ce soldat ici est disposé tout à cette heure de couper votre
gorge.

PIST.   Owy, cuppele gorge, permafoy,
     Peasant, unless thou give me crowns, brave crowns;
     Or mangled shalt thou be by this my sword.

FR. SOL.   O, je vous supplie, pour l'amour de Dieu, me pardonner! Je suis gentilhomme de bonne maison: gardez ma
vie, et je vous donnerai deux cents écus.

PIST.   What are his words?   40

BOY.   He prays you to save his life: he is a gentleman of a good
house; and for his ransom he will give you two hundred
crowns.

PIST.   Tell him my fury shall abate, and I
     The crowns will take.

FR. SOL.   Petit monsieur, que dit-il?

---

19 *O . . . moi!*] O, pardon me!

23 *Écoutez . . . appelé?*] Listen: what's your name?

26 *Master Fer! I'll fer him*] Pistol plays aimlessly on the Frenchman's name.
     firk] beat, thrash.
     ferret him] treat him as the ferret tortures the rabbit.

30 *Que . . . monsieur?*] What is he saying, sir?

31–33 *Il . . . gorge.*] He commands me to tell you to prepare yourself; because this soldier intends to cut your throat right away.

34 *Owy . . . permafoy,*] Yes, cut the throat, by my faith.

37–39 *O, . . . écus.*] O, I beg you to pardon me, for the love of God! I'm a gentleman of
a good breeding: save my life, and I'll give you two hundred crowns.

46 *Petit . . . dit-il?*] Young man, what does he say?

BOY.   Encore qu'il est contre son jurement de pardonner aucun
prisonnier, néanmoins, pour les écus que vous l'avez promis,
il est content de vous donner la liberté, le franchisement.

FR. SOL.   Sur mes genoux je vous donne mille remercîmens; et   50
je m'estime heureux que je suis tombé entre les mains d'un
chevalier, je pense, le plus brave, vaillant, et très distingué
seigneur d'Angleterre.

PIST.   Expound unto me, boy.

BOY.   He gives you, upon his knees, a thousand thanks; and he
esteems himself happy that he hath fallen into the hands of
one, as he thinks, the most brave, valorous, and thrice-wor-
thy signieur of England.

PIST.   As I suck blood, I will some mercy show.
Follow me!   60

BOY.   Suivez-vous le grand capitaine. [*Exeunt* PISTOL, *and*
French Soldier.] I did never know so full a voice issue from
so empty a heart: but the saying is true, "The empty vessel
makes the greatest sound." Bardolph and Nym had ten times
more valour than this roaring devil i' the old play, that every
one may pare his nails with a wooden dagger; and they are
both hanged; and so would this be, if he durst steal any thing
adventurously. I must stay with the lackeys, with the luggage
of our camp: the French might have a good prey of us, if he
knew of it; for there is none to guard it but boys.   [*Exit.*

SCENE V. *Another Part of the Field.*

Enter CONSTABLE, ORLEANS, BOURBON, DAUPHIN, *and*
RAMBURES

CON.   O diable!

ORL.   O Seigneur! le jour est perdu, tout est perdu!

DAU.   Mort de ma vie! all is confounded, all!

47–49 *Encore . . . franchisement.*] Again that it is against his policy to pardon any prisoner. Nonetheless, for the crowns that you've promised, he agrees to give you your
liberty, to set you free.

50–53 *Sur . . . d'Angleterre.*] On my knees I give you a thousand thanks; and I count myself lucky to have fallen into the hands of a knight who, I think, is the bravest, most
valiant, and most distinguished lord of England.

61 *Suivez . . . capitaine.*] Follow the great captain.

65 *devil . . . dagger*] a reference to the Devil (who often carried a wooden dagger) in old
morality plays.

---

2 *O . . . perdu!*] O lord! the day is lost, all is lost!

Reproach and everlasting shame
Sits mocking in our plumes. O méchante fortune!
Do not run away.   [*A short alarum.*

CON.   Why, all our ranks are broke.
DAU.   O perdurable shame! let's stab ourselves.
Be these the wretches that we play'd at dice for?
ORL.   Is this the king we sent to for his ransom?   10
BOUR.   Shame and eternal shame, nothing but shame!
Let us die in honour: once more back again;
And he that will not follow Bourbon now,
Let him go hence, and with his cap in hand,
Like a base pandar, hold the chamber-door
Whilst by a slave, no gentler than my dog,
His fairest daughter is contaminated.
CON.   Disorder, that hath spoil'd us, friend us now!
Let us on heaps go offer up our lives.
ORL.   We are enow yet living in the field   20
To smother up the English in our throngs,
If any order might be thought upon.
BOUR.   The devil take order now! I'll to the throng:
Let life be short; else shame will be too long.   [*Exeunt.*

SCENE VI. *Another Part of the Field.*

Alarum. Enter KING HENRY *and forces*, EXETER, *and others*

K. HEN.   Well have we done, thrice valiant countrymen:
But all's not done; yet keep the French the field.
EXE.   The Duke of York commends him to your majesty.
K. HEN.   Lives he, good uncle? thrice within this hour
I saw him down; thrice up again, and fighting;
From helmet to the spur all blood he was.
EXE.   In which array, brave soldier, doth he lie,
Larding the plain; and by his bloody side,

8 *perdurable*] lasting, eternal.
15 *pandar*] pimp.
16 *no gentler*] of no higher rank.
19 *on heaps*] in crowds, altogether.
20 *enow*] enough.

---

7 *In which array*] In that manner (bloodied "from helmet to spur").
8 *Larding the plain*] Fattening the earth.

Yoke-fellow to his honour-owing wounds,
The noble Earl of Suffolk also lies.   10
Suffolk first died: and York, all haggled over,
Comes to him, where in gore he lay insteep'd,
And takes him by the beard; kisses the gashes
That bloodily did yawn upon his face;
And cries aloud "Tarry, dear cousin Suffolk!
My soul shall thine keep company to heaven;
Tarry, sweet soul, for mine, then fly abreast,
As in this glorious and well-foughten field
We kept together in our chivalry!"
Upon these words I came and cheer'd him up: 20
He smiled me in the face, raught me his hand,
And, with a feeble gripe, says "Dear my lord,
Commend my service to my sovereign."
So did he turn, and over Suffolk's neck
He threw his wounded arm and kiss'd his lips;
And so espoused to death, with blood he seal'd
A testament of noble-ending love.
The pretty and sweet manner of it forced
Those waters from me which I would have stopp'd;
But I had not so much of man in me,   30
And all my mother came into mine eyes
And gave me up to tears.
K. HEN.   I blame you not;
For, hearing this, I must perforce compound
With mistful eyes, or they will issue too.   [*Alarum.*
But, hark! what new alarum is this same?
The French have reinforced their scatter'd men:
Then every soldier kill his prisoners;
Give the word through.   [*Exeunt.*

9 *honour-owing*] honor-owning, honorable.
11 *haggled*] hacked.
21 *raught*] reached.
31 *my mother*] i.e., the more sensitive part of me.
35 *mistful*] growing dim with coming tears.
37 *The French . . . men*] According to some accounts, a few French horsemen suddenly
   raided unguarded tents of the English camp, while the main army was in the field,
   and killed many of the servants; some of the survivors, seized with panic, spread the
   report, which had small foundation, that the French army was regrouping for attack,
   whereupon Henry V gave the order for the slaughter of his French prisoners. In the
   next scene, Gower and Fluellen, upon hearing the rumor that English servant boys
   were killed, express their disgust at the French.

SCENE VII. *Another Part of the Field.*

Enter FLUELLEN *and* GOWER

FLU.   Kill the poys and the luggage! 't is expressly against the law
of arms: 't is as arrant a piece of knavery, mark you now, as
can be offer't; in your conscience, now, is it not?

GOW.   'T is certain there's not a boy left alive; and the cowardly
rascals that ran from the battle ha' done this slaughter: besides, they have burned and carried away all that was in the
king's tent; wherefore the king, most worthily, hath caused
every soldier to cut his prisoner's throat. O, 't is a gallant
king!

FLU.   Ay, he was porn at Monmouth, Captain Gower. What call   10
you the town's name where Alexander the Pig was born?

GOW.   Alexander the Great.

FLU.   Why, I pray you, is not pig great? the pig, or the great, or
the mighty, or the huge, or the magnanimous, are all one
reckonings, save the phrase is a little variations.

GOW.   I think Alexander the Great was born in Macedon: his father was called Philip of Macedon, as I take it.

FLU.   I think it is in Macedon where Alexander is porn. I tell
you, captain, if you look in the maps of the 'orld, I warrant
you sall find, in the comparisons between Macedon and   20
Monmouth, that the situations, look you, is both alike.
There is a river in Macedon; and there is also moreover a
river at Monmouth: it is called Wye at Monmouth; but it is
out of my prains what is the name of the other river; but 't is
all one, 't is alike as my fingers is to my fingers, and there is
salmons in both. If you mark Alexander's life well, Harry of
Monmouth's life is come after it indifferent well; for there is
figures in all things. Alexander, God knows, and you know,
in his rages, and his furies, and his wraths, and his cholers,
and his moods, and his displeasures, and his indignations,   30
and also being a little intoxicates in his prains, did, in his ales
and his angers, look you, kill his best friend, Cleitus.

GOW.   Our king is not like him in that: he never killed any of his
friends.

FLU.   It is not well done, mark you now, to take the tales out of
my mouth, ere it is made and finished. I speak but in the

---

10 *Monmouth*] in Wales, Fluellen's native land.
11 *Pig*] Fluellen's mispronunciation, due to his Welsh accent, of "Big."

figures and comparisons of it: as Alexander killed his friend
Cleitus, being in his ales and his cups; so also Harry Monmouth, being in his right wits and his good judgements,
turned away the fat knight with the great-belly doublet: he   40
was full of jests, and gipes, and knaveries, and mocks; I have
forgot his name.

GOW.   Sir John Falstaff.

FLU.   That is he: I'll tell you there is good men porn at
Monmouth.

GOW.   Here comes his majesty.

Alarum. Enter KING HENRY *and forces;* WARWICK, GLOUCESTER,
EXETER, *and others*

K. HEN.   I was not angry since I came to France
Until this instant. Take a trumpet, herald;
Ride thou unto the horsemen on yon hill:
If they will fight with us, bid them come down,   50
Or void the field; they do offend our sight:
If they'll do neither, we will come to them,
And make them skirr away, as swift as stones
Enforced from the old Assyrian slings:
Besides, we'll cut the throats of those we have,
And not a man of them that we shall take
Shall taste our mercy. Go and tell them so.

Enter MONTJOY

EXE.   Here comes the herald of the French, my liege.

GLOU.   His eyes are humbler than they used to be.

K. HEN.   How now! what means this, herald? know'st thou not   60
That I have fined these bones of mine for ransom?
Comest thou again for ransom?

MONT.   No, great king:
I come to thee for charitable license,
That we may wander o'er this bloody field
To book our dead, and then to bury them;
To sort our nobles from our common men.
For many of our princes—woe the while!—
Lie drown'd and soak'd in mercenary blood;

53 *skirr*] scurry.
61 *fined*] agreed to pay as fine.
66 *book*] register.

So do our vulgar drench their peasant limbs 70
In blood of princes; and their wounded steeds
Fret fetlock deep in gore, and with wild rage
Yerk out their armed heels at their dead masters,
Killing them twice. O, give us leave, great king,
To view the field in safety and dispose
Of their dead bodies!

K. HEN.   I tell thee truly, herald,
I know not if the day be ours or no;
For yet a many of your horsemen peer
And gallop o'er the field. 80

MONT.   The day is yours.

K. HEN.   Praised be God, and not our strength, for it!
What is this castle call'd that stands hard by?

MONT.   They call it Agincourt.

K. HEN.   Then call we this the field of Agincourt,
Fought on the day of Crispin Crispianus.

FLU.   Your grandfather of famous memory, an 't please your
majesty, and your great-uncle Edward the Plack Prince of
Wales, as I have read in the chronicles, fought a most prave
pattle here in France. 90

K. HEN.   They did, Fluellen.

FLU.   Your majesty says very true: if your majesties is remembered of it, the Welshmen did good service in a garden
where leeks did grow, wearing leeks in their Monmouth
caps; which, your majesty know, to this hour is an hon-
ourable badge of the service; and I do believe your majesty
takes no scorn to wear the leek upon Saint Tavy's day.

K. HEN.   I wear it for a memorable honour;
For I am Welsh, you know, good countryman.

FLU.   All the water in Wye cannot wash your majesty's Welsh 100
plood out of your pody, I can tell you that: God pless it and
preserve it, as long as it pleases his grace, and his majesty
too!

K. HEN.   Thanks, good my countryman.

FLU.   By Jeshu, I am your majesty's countryman, I care not who

70 *vulgar*] commoners.
73 *Yerk*] Jerk, kick.
83 *hard by*] nearby.
86 *Crispin Crispianus*] See IV, iii, 42.
87 *an 't*] if it.
94–95 *Monmouth caps*] Caps made at Monmouth were considered to be of the best
quality.

know it; I will confess it to all the 'orld: I need not to be
ashamed of your majesty, praised be God, so long as your
majesty is an honest man.

K. HEN.   God keep me so! Our heralds go with him:
Bring me just notice of the numbers dead   110
On both our parts. Call yonder fellow hither.

> [*Points to* WILLIAMS. *Exeunt* Heralds *with* MONTJOY.

EXE.   Soldier, you must come to the king.

K. HEN.   Soldier, why wearest thou that glove in thy cap?

WILL.   An 't please your majesty, 't is the gage of one that I
should fight withal, if he be alive.

K. HEN.   An Englishman?

WILL.   An 't please your majesty, a rascal that swaggered with me
last night; who, if alive and ever dare to challenge this glove,
I have sworn to take him a box o' th' ear: or if I can see my
glove in his cap, which he swore, as he was a soldier, he   120
would wear if alive, I will strike it out soundly.

K. HEN.   What think you, Captain Fluellen? is it fit this soldier
keep his oath?

FLU.   He is a craven and a villain else, an 't please your majesty,
in my conscience.

K. HEN.   It may be his enemy is a gentleman of great sort, quite
from the answer of his degree.

FLU.   Though he be as good a gentleman as the devil is, as
Lucifer and Belzebub himself, it is necessary, look your
grace, that he keep his vow and his oath: if he be perjured,   130
see you now, his reputation is as arrant a villain and a
Jacksauce, as ever his black shoe trod upon God's ground
and his earth, in my conscience, la!

K. HEN.   Then keep thy vow, sirrah, when thou meetest the fellow.

WILL.   So I will, my liege, as I live.

K. HEN.   Who servest thou under?

---

113 *Soldier . . . cap*] See IV, i, 186–199, for the quarrel between Williams and King
   Henry, who was disguised as a commoner. Williams still does not realize that he
   made the challenge to his king.
126–127 *a gentleman . . . degree*] a gentleman of such high rank as not to allow him to
   answer a challenge from one of the soldiers of low degree.
132 *a Jacksauce*] a saucy Jack; a common term of contempt.

Will.　Under Captain Gower, my liege.

Flu.　Gower is a good captain, and is good knowledge and liter-
atured in the wars.　　　　　　　　　　　　　　　　　　　　140

K. Hen.　Call him hither to me, soldier.

Will.　I will, my liege.　　　　　　　　　　　　　　　[*Exit.*

K. Hen.　Here, Fluellen; wear thou this favour for me and stick
it in thy cap: when Alençon and myself were down together,
I plucked this glove from his helm: if any man challenge
this, he is a friend to Alençon, and an enemy to our person;
if thou encounter any such, apprehend him, an thou dost
me love.

Flu.　Your grace doo's me as great honours as can be desired in
the hearts of his subjects: I would fain see the man, that has　150
but two legs, that shall find himself aggriefed at this glove;
that is all; but I would fain see it once, an 't please God of
his grace that I might see.

K. Hen.　Knowest thou Gower?

Flu.　He is my dear friend, an 't please you.

K. Hen.　Pray thee, go seek him, and bring him to my tent.

Flu.　I will fetch him.　　　　　　　　　　　　　　　[*Exit.*

K. Hen.　My Lord of Warwick, and my brother Gloucester,
Follow Fluellen closely at the heels:
The glove which I have given him for a favour　　　　　　160
May haply purchase him a box o' th' ear;
It is the soldier's; I by bargain should
Wear it myself. Follow, good cousin Warwick:
If that the soldier strike him, as I judge
By his blunt bearing he will keep his word,
Some sudden mischief may arise of it;
For I do know Fluellen valiant,
And, touch'd with choler, hot as gunpowder,
And quickly will return an injury:
Follow, and see there be no harm between them.　　　　170
Go you with me, uncle of Exeter.　　　　　　　　　[*Exeunt.*

---

144 *Alençon*] This alludes to a legendary encounter between the king and the Duke of
Alençon in the course of the battle of Agincourt. The king was almost felled by the
duke, but he succeeded in striking the Frenchman down, and in killing two of the
duke's companions. The duke himself was killed by the king's guard.

145 *helm*] helmet.

150 *fain*] willingly.

168 *touch'd with choler*] hot-tempered.

SCENE VIII. *Before King Henry's Pavilion.*

Enter GOWER *and* WILLIAMS

WILL.   I warrant it is to knight you, captain.

Enter FLUELLEN

FLU.   God's will and his pleasure, captain, I beseech you now,
come apace to the king: there is more good toward you peradventure than is in your knowledge to dream of.

WILL.   Sir, know you this glove?

FLU.   Know the glove! I know the glove is a glove.

WILL.   I know this; and thus I challenge it.   [*Strikes him.*

FLU.   'Sblood! an arrant traitor as any is in the universal world,
or in France, or in England!

GOW.   How now, sir! you villain!   10

WILL.   Do you think I'll be forsworn?

FLU.   Stand away, Captain Gower; I will give treason his payment into plows, I warrant you.

WILL.   I am no traitor.

FLU.   That's a lie in thy throat. I charge you in his majesty's
name, apprehend him: he's a friend of the Duke Alençon's.

Enter WARWICK *and* GLOUCESTER

WAR.   How now, how now! what's the matter?

FLU.   My Lord of Warwick, here is—praised be God for it!—a
most contagious treason come to light, look you, as you shall
desire in a summer's day. Here is his majesty.   20

Enter KING HENRY *and* EXETER

K. HEN.   How now! what's the matter?

FLU.   My liege, here is a villain and a traitor, that, look your
grace, has struck the glove which your majesty is take out of
the helmet of Alençon.

WILL.   My liege, this was my glove; here is the fellow of it; and
he that I gave it to in change promised to wear it in his cap:
I promised to strike him, if he did: I met this man with my
glove in his cap, and I have been as good as my word.

FLU.   Your majesty hear now, saving your majesty's manhood,

3 *apace*] at once.
13 *into plows*] in blows, punches.
19 *contagious*] blunder for "outrageous."
26 *in change*] in exchange.

what an arrant, rascally, beggarly, lousy knave it is: I hope   30
your majesty is pear me testimony and witness, and will
avouchment, that this is the glove of Alençon, that your
majesty is give me; in your conscience, now.

K. HEN.   Give me thy glove, soldier: look, here is the fellow of
it.
'T was I, indeed, thou promised'st to strike;
And thou hast given me most bitter terms.

FLU.   And please your majesty, let his neck answer for it, if there
is any martial law in the world.

K. HEN.   How canst thou make me satisfaction?   40

WILL.   All offences, my lord, come from the heart: never came
any from mine that might offend your majesty.

K. HEN.   It was ourself thou didst abuse.

WILL.   Your majesty came not like yourself: you appeared to me
but as a common man; witness the night, your garments,
your lowliness; and what your highness suffered under that
shape, I beseech you to take it for your own fault and not
mine: for had you been as I took you for, I made no offence;
therefore, I beseech your highness, pardon me.

K. HEN.   Here, uncle Exeter, fill this glove with crowns,   50
And give it to this fellow. Keep it, fellow;
And wear it for an honour in thy cap
Till I do challenge it. Give him the crowns:
And, captain, you must needs be friends with him.

FLU.   By this day and this light, the fellow has mettle enough in
his belly. Hold, there is twelve pence for you; and I pray you
to serve God, and keep you out of prawls, and prabbles, and
quarrels, and dissensions, and, I warrant you, it is the better
for you.

WILL.   I will none of your money.   60

FLU.   It is with a good will; I can tell you, it will serve you to
mend your shoes: come, wherefore should you be so pash-
ful? your shoes is not so good: 't is a good silling, I warrant
you, or I will change it.

Enter an English Herald

K. HEN.   Now, herald, are the dead number'd?

HER.   Here is the number of the slaughter'd French.

K. HEN.   What prisoners of good sort are taken, uncle?

31 *is pear*] will bear.
32 *avouchment*] avouch, affirm.
46 *lowliness*] humble appearance.

EXE.   Charles Duke of Orleans, nephew to the king;
     John Duke of Bourbon, and Lord Bouciqualt:
     Of other lords and barons, knights and squires,   70
     Full fifteen hundred, besides common men.
K. HEN.   This note doth tell me of ten thousand French
     That in the field lie slain: of princes, in this number,
     And nobles bearing banners, there lie dead
     One hundred twenty six: added to these,
     Of knights, esquires, and gallant gentlemen,
     Eight thousand and four hundred; of the which,
     Five hundred were but yesterday dubb'd knights:
     So that, in these ten thousand they have lost,
     There are but sixteen hundred mercenaries;   80
     The rest are princes, barons, lords, knights, squires,
     And gentlemen of blood and quality.
     The names of those their nobles that lie dead:
     Charles Delabreth, high constable of France;
     Jaques of Chatillon, admiral of France;
     The master of the cross-bows, Lord Rambures;
     Great Master of France, the brave Sir Guichard Dolphin,
     John Duke of Alençon, Anthony Duke of Brabant,
     The brother to the Duke of Burgundy,
     And Edward Duke of Bar: of lusty earls,   90
     Grandpré and Roussi, Fauconberg and Foix,
     Beaumont and Marle, Vaudemont and Lestrale.
     Here was a royal fellowship of death!
     Where is the number of our English dead?
                     [Herald *shews him another paper.*
     Edward the Duke of York, the Earl of Suffolk,
     Sir Richard Ketly, Davy Gam, esquire:
     None else of name; and of all other men
     But five and twenty. O God, thy arm was here;
     And not to us, but to thy arm alone,
     Ascribe we all! When, without stratagem,   100
     But in plain shock and even play of battle,
     Was ever known so great and little loss
     On one part and on th' other? Take it, God,
     For it is none but thine!

---

96 *Davy Gam*] David Gam or Ab Llewelyn, a Welsh warrior who, it is recorded, was
    ordered to discover the strength of the enemy and reported to the king "There are
    enough to be killed, enough to take prisoners, and enough to run away."
101 *shock*] confrontation.
    even] equal.

EXE.   'T is wonderful!

K. HEN.   Come, go we in procession to the village:
   And be it death proclaimed through our host
   To boast of this or take that praise from God
   Which is his only.

FLU.   Is it not lawful, an 't please your majesty, to tell how many   110
   is killed?

K. HEN.   Yes, captain; but with this acknowledgement,
   That God fought for us.

FLU.   Yes, my conscience, he did us great good.

K. HEN.   Do we all holy rites;
   Let there be sung "Non nobis" and "Te Deum";
   The dead with charity enclosed in clay:
   And then to Calais; and to England then;
   Where ne'er from France arrived more happy men.

                                          [*Exeunt.*

---

116 *Non nobis*] reference to Psalm 115, which begins, "Not unto us, O Lord, not unto
   us, but unto thy name give glory."
   Te Deum] a hymn of thanksgiving, which begins "We praise thee O God."

ACT V. — PROLOGUE

Enter Chorus

CHORUS.   Vouchsafe to those that have not read the story,
That I may prompt them: and of such as have,
I humbly pray them to admit the excuse
Of time, of numbers and due course of things,
Which cannot in their huge and proper life
Be here presented. Now we bear the king
Toward Calais: grant him there; there seen,
Heave him away upon your winged thoughts
Athwart the sea. Behold, the English beach
Pales in the flood with men, with wives and boys,   10
Whose shouts and claps out-voice the deep-mouth'd sea,
Which like a mighty whiffler 'fore the king
Seems to prepare his way: so let him land,
And solemnly see him set on to London.
So swift a pace hath thought, that even now
You may imagine him upon Blackheath;
Where that his lords desire him to have borne
His bruised helmet and his bended sword
Before him through the city: he forbids it,
Being free from vainness and self-glorious pride;   20
Giving full trophy, signal and ostent
Quite from himself to God. But now behold,

3–6 *admit the excuse . . . presented*] excuse, in the interests of time, that we cannot tell
  the entire story.
10 *Pales in the flood*] surrounds the sea.
12 *whiffler*] an officer who marches at the head of a procession to clear the way.
14 *solemnly . . . set on*] in solemn state . . . set forth.
16 *Blackheath*] area just outside of London.
21–22 *Giving full trophy . . . to God*] Transferring all credit for the trophies, signs, and
  outward show of the victory from himself to God.

In the quick forge and working-house of thought,
How London doth pour out her citizens!
The mayor and all his brethren in best sort,
Like to the senators of the antique Rome,
With the plebeians swarming at their heels,
Go forth and fetch their conquering Cæsar in:
As, by a lower but loving likelihood,
Were now the general of our gracious empress,   30
As in good time he may, from Ireland coming,
Bringing rebellion broached on his sword,
How many would the peaceful city quit,
To welcome him! much more, and much more cause,
Did they this Harry. Now in London place him;
As yet the lamentation of the French
Invites the King of England's stay at home;
The emperor's coming in behalf of France,
To order peace between them; and omit
All the occurrences, whatever chanced,   40
Till Harry's back return again to France:
There must we bring him; and myself have play'd
The interim, by remembering you 't is past.
Then brook abridgement, and your eyes advance,
After your thoughts, straight back again to France.   [*Exit.*

25 *in best sort*] in best array.

29 *by a lower . . . likelihood*] to take a similar event, of inferior importance, but exciting no less affectionate emotion.

30–32 *Were now . . . his sword*] This is a reference to Robert Devereux, second earl of Essex, Queen Elizabeth's favorite, who was at the time of the production of this play lord deputy of Ireland and was engaged in repressing a native rebellion. He had passed through London on 27 March 1599, on his way to Ireland, and had been accorded a great popular ovation. Shakespeare's anticipation of his triumphant return was not realized. His government of Ireland proved a failure, and he came home in September in disgrace.

32 *broached*] spitted, transfixed.

38–39 *The emperor's coming . . . between them*] The Holy Roman Emperor came to England in May 1416 to mediate between England and France. The emperor was unsuccessful, the war between the French and English continued, and King Henry traveled once again back to France.

SCENE I. *France—The English Camp.*

Enter FLUELLEN *and* GOWER

GOW.   Nay, that's right; but why wear you your leek to-day?
Saint Davy's day is past.

FLU.   There is occasions and causes why and wherefore in all
things: I will tell you, asse my friend, Captain Gower: the
rascally, scauld, beggarly, lousy, pragging knave, Pistol,
which you and yourself and all the world know to be no petter than a fellow, look you now, of no merits, he is come to
me and prings me pread and salt yesterday, look you, and bid
me eat my leek: it was in a place where I could not breed no
contention with him; but I will be so bold as to wear it in my   10
cap till I see him once again, and then I will tell him a little
piece of my desires.

Enter PISTOL

GOW.   Why, here he comes, swelling like a turkey-cock.

FLU.   'T is no matter for his swellings nor his turkey-cocks. God
pless you, Aunchient Pistol! you scurvy, lousy knave, God
pless you.

PIST.   Ha! art thou bedlam? dost thou thirst, base Trojan,
To have me fold up Parca's fatal web?
Hence! I am qualmish at the smell of leek.

FLU.   I peseech you heartily, scurvy, lousy knave, at my desires,   20
and my requests, and my petitions, to eat, look you, this leek:
because, look you, you do not love it, nor your affections and
your appetites and your digestions doo's not agree with it, I
would desire you to eat it.

PIST.   Not for Cadwallader and all his goats.

FLU.   There is one goat for you. [*Strikes him.*] Will you be so
good, scauld knave, as eat it?

---

4 *asse*] mispronounciation of "as."

5 *scauld*] scabby; a low word of contempt, implying filth.

6–7 *petter*] mispronunciation of "better."

17 *art thou bedlam*] art thou a madman.

    Trojan] i.e., rascal.

18 *fold up Parca's fatal web*] end thy life.

19 *qualmish*] squeamish, nauseated.

25 *Cadwallader*] a former king of Wales.

    all his goats] Pistol insults Fluellen with the English taunt that the Welsh are no
more than common goatherders.

PIST.   Base Trojan, thou shalt die.

FLU.   You say very true, scauld knave, when God's will is: I will
       desire you to live in the mean time, and eat your victuals: 30
       come, there is sauce for it. [*Strikes him.*] You called me yes-
       terday mountain-squire; but I will make you to-day a squire
       of low degree. I pray you, fall to: if you can mock a leek, you
       can eat a leek.

GOW.   Enough, captain: you have astonished him.

FLU.   I say, I will make him eat some part of my leek, or I will
       peat his pate four days. Bite, I pray you; it is good for your
       green wound and your ploody coxcomb.

PIST.   Must I bite?

FLU.   Yes, certainly, and out of doubt and out of question too,   40
       and ambiguities.

PIST.   By this leek, I will most horribly revenge: I eat and eat, I
       swear—

FLU.   Eat, I pray you: will you have some more sauce to your
       leek? there is not enough leek to swear by.

PIST.   Quiet thy cudgel; thou dost see I eat.

FLU.   Much good do you, scauld knave, heartily. Nay, pray you,
       throw none away; the skin is good for your broken coxcomb.
       When you take occasions to see leeks hereafter, I pray you,
       mock at 'em; that is all.   50

PIST.   Good.

FLU.   Ay, leeks is good: hold you, there is a groat to heal your
       pate.

PIST.   Me a groat!

FLU.   Yes, verily and in truth, you shall take it; or I have another
       leek in my pocket, which you shall eat.

PIST.   I take thy groat in earnest of revenge.

FLU.   If I owe you any thing, I will pay you in cudgels: you shall
       be a woodmonger, and buy nothing of me but cudgels. God
       b' wi' you, and keep you, and heal your pate.   [*Exit.* 60

PIST.   All hell shall stir for this.

GOW.   Go, go; you are a counterfeit cowardly knave. Will you
       mock at an ancient tradition, begun upon an honourable
       respect, and worn as a memorable trophy of predeceased

---

35 *astonished him*] put him into a panic.
37 *peat his pate*] beat his head.
38 *coxcomb*] fool's head.
46 *Quiet thy cudgel*] Put down your weapon, stop with your threats.
52 *groat*] coin of little value.
59 *a woodmonger*] a dealer in wood.

valour, and dare not avouch in your deeds any of your
words? I have seen you gleeking and galling at this gentleman twice or thrice. You thought, because he could not
speak English in the native garb, he could not therefore handle an English cudgel: you find it otherwise; and henceforth
let a Welsh correction teach you a good English condition.   70
Fare ye well.

                                                 [*Exit.*

PIST.   Doth Fortune play the huswife with me now?
     News have I, that my Doll is dead i' the spital
     Of malady of France;
     And there my rendezvous is quite cut off.
     Old I do wax; and from my weary limbs
     Honour is cudgelled. Well, bawd I'll turn,
     And something lean to cutpurse of quick hand.
     To England will I steal, and there I'll steal:
     And patches will I get unto these cudgell'd scars,   80
     And swear I got them in the Gallia wars.   [*Exit.*

SCENE II. *France—A Royal Palace.*

Enter, at one door, KING HENRY, EXETER, BEDFORD,
     GLOUCESTER, WARWICK, WESTMORELAND, *and other* Lords;
     at another, the FRENCH KING, QUEEN ISABEL, *the* PRINCESS
     KATHARINE, ALICE *and other* Ladies; *the* DUKE OF
     BURGUNDY, *and his train*

K. HEN.   Peace to this meeting, wherefore we are met!
     Unto our brother France, and to our sister,
     Health and fair time of day; joy and good wishes
     To our most fair and princely cousin Katharine;
     And, as a branch and member of this royalty,

66 *gleeking and galling*] gibing or sneering and mocking.
70 *condition*] behavior, manners.
72 *huswife*] hussy, jilt.
73–74 *News . . . of France*] Pistol has learned that his wife died in the hospital of a vene-
     real disease. "Doll" is Shakespeare's error for "Nell," Mrs. Quickly's first name. (See
     above, II, i, 15.)
75 *rendezvous*] refuge.
76 *wax*] become.
78 *something lean to cutpurse*] become a pickpocket.
81 *Gallia*] French.

1 *Peace . . . met*] Peace, for making which we have met, be to this meeting.

> By whom this great assembly is contrived,
> We do salute you, Duke of Burgundy;
> And, princes French, and peers, health to you all!

FR. KING.　Right joyous are we to behold your face,
> Most worthy brother England; fairly met:　　　　　　10
> So are you, princes English, every one.

Q. ISA.　So happy be the issue, brother England,
> Of this good day and of this gracious meeting,
> As we are now glad to behold your eyes;
> Your eyes, which hitherto have borne in them
> Against the French, that met them in their bent,
> The fatal balls of murdering basilisks:
> The venom of such looks, we fairly hope,
> Have lost their quality, and that this day
> Shall change all griefs and quarrels into love.　　　20

K. HEN.　To cry amen to that, thus we appear.

Q. ISA.　You English princes all, I do salute you.

BUR.　My duty to you both, on equal love,
> Great Kings of France and England! That I have labour'd,
> With all my wits, my pains and strong endeavours,
> To bring your most imperial majesties
> Unto this bar and royal interview,
> Your mightiness on both parts best can witness.
> Since then my office hath so far prevail'd
> That, face to face and royal eye to eye,　　　　　　30
> You have congreeted, let it not disgrace me,
> If I demand, before this royal view,
> What rub or what impediment there is,
> Why that the naked, poor and mangled Peace,
> Dear nurse of arts, plenties and joyful births,
> Should not in this best garden of the world,
> Our fertile France, put up her lovely visage?
> Alas, she hath from France too long been chased,
> And all her husbandry doth lie on heaps,
> Corrupting in its own fertility.　　　　　　　　　40
> Her vine, the merry cheerer of the heart,

16 *in their bent*] in their sight.
17 *basilisks*] meaning both large cannons and the fabulous serpents that killed men by
　　their gaze.
27 *bar*] tribunal.
31 *congreeted*] greeted each other, come together.
33 *rub*] obstacle.
39 *husbandry*] farmlands.

Unpruned dies; her hedges even-pleach'd,
Like prisoners wildly overgrown with hair,
Put forth disorder'd twigs; her fallow leas
The darnel, hemlock and rank fumitory
Doth root upon, while that the coulter rusts
That should deracinate such savagery;
The even mead, that erst brought sweetly forth
The freckled cowslip, burnet and green clover,
Wanting the scythe, all uncorrected, rank,   50
Conceives by idleness, and nothing teems
But hateful docks, rough thistles, kecksies, burs,
Losing both beauty and utility.
And as our vineyards, fallows, meads and hedges,
Defective in their natures, grow to wildness,
Even so our houses and ourselves and children
Have lost, or do not learn for want of time,
The sciences that should become our country;
But grow like savages,—as soldiers will
That nothing do but meditate on blood,—   60
To swearing and stern looks, diffused attire
And every thing that seems unnatural.
Which to reduce into our former favour
You are assembled: and my speech entreats
That I may know the let, why gentle Peace
Should not expel these inconveniences
And bless us with her former qualities.
K. HEN.   If, Duke of Burgundy, you would the peace,
Whose want gives growth to the imperfections
Which you have cited, you must buy that peace   70
With full accord to all our just demands;

42 *even-pleach'd*] matted together, thickly interwoven.
44 *fallow leas*] uncultivated fields.
45 *darnel . . . fumitory*] various types of weeds.
46 *coulter*] the blade of the ploughshare.
47 *deracinate*] root out.
49 *burnet*] a sweet-smelling salad plant.
51 *teems*] grows.
52 *docks*] coarse weeds.
   kecksies] hemlock stalks.
55 *Defective in their natures*] Failing in their proper virtues.
61 *diffused attire*] dishevelled dress.
63 *reduce into . . . favour*] return to our former good appearance.
65 *let*] obstacle.
68 *would*] wish.

Whose tenours and particular effects
You have enscheduled briefly in your hands.
BUR.   The king hath heard them; to the which as yet
There is no answer made.
K. HEN.   Well then the peace,
Which you before so urged, lies in his answer.
FR. KING.   I have but with a cursorary eye
O'erglanced the articles: pleaseth your grace
To appoint some of your council presently   80
To sit with us once more, with better heed
To re-survey them, we will suddenly
Pass our accept and peremptory answer.
K. HEN.   Brother, we shall. Go, uncle Exeter,
And brother Clarence, and you, brother Gloucester,
Warwick and Huntingdon, go with the king;
And take with you free power to ratify,
Augment, or alter, as your wisdoms best
Shall see advantageable for our dignity,
Any thing in or out of our demands;   90
And we'll consign thereto. Will you, fair sister,
Go with the princes, or stay here with us?
Q. ISA.   Our gracious brother, I will go with them:
Haply a woman's voice may do some good,
When articles too nicely urged be stood on.
K. HEN.   Yet leave our cousin Katharine here with us:
She is our capital demand, comprised
Within the fore-rank of our articles.
Q. ISA.   She hath good leave.

        [*Exeunt all except* HENRY, KATHARINE, *and* ALICE.

K. HEN.   Fair Katharine, and most fair,   100
Will you vouchsafe to teach a soldier terms
Such as will enter at a lady's ear
And plead his love-suit to her gentle heart?

72 *tenours and particular effects*] essence and details.
73 *enscheduled*] presented in writing.
78 *cursorary*] cursory, hasty.
82–83 *we will suddenly . . . answer*] we will immediately determine our definite and final
    answer.
91 *consign*] agree.
94 *Haply*] Perhaps.
95 *When . . . stood on*] When trivial matters are senselessly insisted on.
97 *capital*] most important.
98 *fore-rank of our articles*] first part of our listed demands.

KATH. Your majesty shall mock at me; I cannot speak your England.

K. HEN. O fair Katharine, if you will love me soundly with your French heart, I will be glad to hear you confess it brokenly with your English tongue. Do you like me, Kate?

KATH. Pardonnez-moi, I cannot tell vat is "like me."

K. HEN. An angel is like you, Kate, and you are like an angel.   110

KATH. Que dit-il? que je suis semblable à les anges?

ALICE. Oui, vraiment, sauf votre grace, ainsi dit-il.

K. HEN. I said so, dear Katharine; and I must not blush to affirm it.

KATH. O bon Dieu! les langues des hommes sont pleines de tromperies.

K. HEN. What says she, fair one? that the tongues of men are full of deceits?

ALICE. Oui, dat de tongues of de mans is be full of deceits: dat is de princess.   120

K. HEN. The princess is the better Englishwoman. I' faith, Kate, my wooing is fit for thy understanding: I am glad thou canst speak no better English; for, if thou couldst, thou wouldst find me such a plain king that thou wouldst think I had sold my farm to buy my crown. I know no ways to mince it in love, but directly to say "I love you:" then if you urge me farther than to say "Do you in faith?" I wear out my suit. Give me your answer; i' faith, do: and so clap hands and a bargain: how say you, lady?

KATH. Sauf votre honneur, me understand vell.   130

K. HEN. Marry, if you would put me to verses or to dance for your sake, Kate, why you undid me: for the one, I have neither words nor measure, and for the other, I have no strength in measure, yet a reasonable measure in strength. If I could win a lady at leap-frog, or by vaulting into my saddle with my

---

111 *Que . . . anges?*] What does he say? that I'm like the angels?

112 *Oui, . . . dit-il.*] Yes, truly, save your grace, that's what he says.

115–116 *O . . . tromperies.*] O good God! Men's tongues are full of lies!

119–120 *dat is de princess*] The meaning may be "that is the princess's opinion." The sentence may possibly be interrupted by the king.

121 *the better Englishwoman*] i.e., she has a real Englishwoman's modesty and suspicion of flattery.

124 *plain*] unaffected, straightforward.

127 *I wear out my suit*] I have nothing more to add.

128 *clap*] clasp.

132 *you undid me*] you would defeat me.

133–134 *measure . . . measure . . . measure*] meter . . . dancing . . . amount.

armour on my back, under the correction of bragging be it
spoken, I should quickly leap into a wife. Or if I might buffet for my love, or bound my horse for her favours, I could
lay on like a butcher and sit like a jack-an-apes, never off.
But, before God, Kate, I cannot look greenly nor gasp out   140
my eloquence, nor I have no cunning in protestation; only
downright oaths, which I never use till urged, nor never
break for urging. If thou canst love a fellow of this temper,
Kate, whose face is not worth sun-burning, that never looks
in his glass for love of any thing he sees there, let thine eye
be thy cook. I speak to thee plain soldier: if thou canst love
me for this, take me; if not, to say to thee that I shall die, is
true; but for thy love, by the Lord, no; yet I love thee too.
And while thou livest, dear Kate, take a fellow of plain and
uncoined constancy; for he perforce must do thee right, be-   150
cause he hath not the gift to woo in other places: for these
fellows of infinite tongue, that can rhyme themselves into
ladies' favours, they do always reason themselves out again.
What! a speaker is but a prater; a rhyme is but a ballad. A
good leg will fall; a straight back will stoop; a black beard
will turn white; a curled pate will grow bald; a fair face will
wither; a full eye will wax hollow: but a good heart, Kate, is
the sun and the moon; or, rather, the sun, and not the moon;
for it shines bright and never changes, but keeps his course
truly. If thou would have such a one, take me; and take me,   160
take a soldier; take a soldier, take a king. And what sayest
thou then to my love? speak, my fair, and fairly, I pray thee.

KATH.   Is it possible dat I sould love de enemy of France?

K. HEN.   No; it is not possible you should love the enemy of
France, Kate: but, in loving me, you should love the friend
of France; for I love France so well that I will not part with
a village of it; I will have it all mine: and, Kate, when France
is mine and I am yours, then yours is France and you are
mine.

---

137 *buffet*] fight, box.
139 *sit like a jack-an-apes*] sit tight like a monkey.
140 *look greenly*] look like a nervous young lover.
144 *not worth sun-burning*] i.e., so ugly that even the sun couldn't make it worse.
145–146 *let thine eye . . . cook*] let thy gaze fashion me to thy fancy.
149–150 *of plain and uncoined constancy*] as of plain sterling metal, which has not yet
    been stamped or manipulated for circulation as coinage.
150 *perforce must*] is compelled to.
155 *fall*] fall away, shrink.

KATH. I cannot tell vat is dat.   170

K. HEN. No, Kate? I will tell thee in French; which I am sure will hang upon my tongue like a new-married wife about her husband's neck, hardly to be shook off. Je quand sur le possession de France, et quand vous avez le possession de moi, — let me see, what then? Saint Denis be my speed! — donc votre est France et vous êtes mienne. It is as easy for me, Kate, to conquer the kingdom as to speak so much more French: I shall never move thee in French, unless it be to laugh at me.

KATH. Sauf votre honneur, le François que vous parlez, il est   180 meilleur que l'Anglois lequel je parle.

K. HEN. No, faith, is 't not, Kate: but thy speaking of my tongue, and I thine, most truly-falsely, must needs be granted to be much at one. But, Kate, dost thou understand thus much English, canst thou love me?

KATH. I cannot tell.

K. HEN. Can any of your neighbours tell, Kate? I'll ask them. Come, I know thou lovest me: and at night, when you come into your closet, you'll question this gentlewoman about me; and I know, Kate, you will to her dispraise those parts in me   190 that you love with your heart: but, good Kate, mock me mercifully; the rather, gentle princess, because I love thee cruelly. If ever thou beest mine, Kate, as I have a saving faith within me tells me thou shalt, I get thee with scambling, and thou must therefore needs prove a good soldier-breeder: shall not thou and I, between Saint Denis and Saint George, compound a boy, half French, half English, that shall go to Constantinople and take the Turk by the beard? shall we not? what sayest thou, my fair flower-de-luce?

KATH. I do not know dat.   200

173–176 *Je quand . . . mienne.*] When I have possession of France, and you have possession of me . . . then France is yours and you are mine.

175 *Saint Denis*] patron saint of France.

180–181 *Sauf . . . parle.*] Save your honor, the French that you speak is better than the English that I speak.

183 *truly-falsely*] expressed truthfully but incorrectly.

184 *much at one*] much alike.

189 *closet*] private chamber.

192–193 *cruelly*] intensely.

194 *scambling*] struggling, fighting.

199 *flower-de-luce*] lily, fleur-de-lys, the emblem of the French monarchy.

K. HEN.   No; 't is hereafter to know, but now to promise: do but
now promise, Kate, you will endeavour for your French part
of such a boy; and for my English moiety take the word of a
king and a bachelor. How answer you, la plus belle
Katharine du monde, mon très cher et devin déesse?

KATH.   Your majestee ave fausse French enough to deceive de
most sage demoiselle dat is en France.

K. HEN.   Now, fie upon my false French! By mine honour, in
true English, I love thee, Kate: by which honour I dare not
swear thou lovest me; yet my blood begins to flatter me that   210
thou dost, notwithstanding the poor and untempering effect
of my visage. Now, beshrew my father's ambition! he was
thinking of civil wars when he got me: therefore was I cre-
ated with a stubborn outside, with an aspect of iron, that,
when I come to woo ladies, I fright them. But, in faith, Kate,
the elder I wax, the better I shall appear: my comfort is, that
old age, that ill layer up of beauty, can do no more spoil
upon my face: thou hast me, if thou hast me, at the worst;
and thou shalt wear me, if thou wear me, better and better:
and therefore tell me, most fair Katharine, will you have me?   220
Put off your maiden blushes; avouch the thoughts of your
heart with the looks of an empress; take me by the hand, and
say "Harry of England, I am thine": which word thou shalt
no sooner bless mine ear withal, but I will tell thee aloud
"England is thine, Ireland is thine, France is thine, and
Henry Plantagenet is thine"; who, though I speak it before
his face, if he be not fellow with the best king, thou shalt find
the best king of good fellows. Come, your answer in broken
music; for thy voice is music and thy English broken; therefore, queen of all, Katharine, break thy mind to me in bro-   230
ken English, wilt thou have me?

KATH.   Dat is as it sall please de roi mon père.

---

203 *moiety*] half.
204–205 *la plus . . . déesse?*] . . . the most beautiful Katharine in the world, my very dear
and divine goddess?
206 *fausse*] false, i.e., both "incorrect" and "deceptive."
211 *untempering effect*] unsoftening, unconciliatory quality.
212 *beshrew*] curse.
216 *wax*] grow, age.
221 *avouch*] acknowledge.
232 *Dat . . . père*] i.e., That's up to my father the king.

K. HEN.   Nay, it will please him well, Kate; it shall please him, Kate.

KATH.   Den it sall also content me.

K. HEN.   Upon that I kiss your hand, and I call you my queen.

KATH.   Laissez, mon seigneur, laissez, laissez: ma foi, je ne veux point que vous abaissiez votre grandeur en baisant la main d'une de votre seigneurie indigne serviteur; excusez-moi, je vous supplie, mon très-puissant seigneur.   240

K. HEN.   Then I will kiss your lips, Kate.

KATH.   Les dames et demoiselles pour être baisées devant leur noces, il n'est pas la coutume de France.

K. HEN.   Madam, my interpreter, what says she?

ALICE.   Dat it is not be de fashion pour les ladies of France,—I cannot tell vat is baiser en Anglish.

K. HEN.   To kiss.

ALICE.   Your majesty entendre bettre que moi.

K. HEN.   It is not a fashion for the maids in France to kiss before they are married, would she say?   250

ALICE.   Oui, vraiment.

K. HEN.   O Kate, nice customs courtesy to great kings. Dear Kate, you and I cannot be confined within the weak list of a country's fashion: we are the makers of manners, Kate; and the liberty that follows our places stops the mouth of all find-faults; as I will do yours, for upholding the nice fashion of your country in denying me a kiss: therefore, patiently and yielding. [*Kissing her.*] You have witchcraft in your lips, Kate: there is more eloquence in a sugar touch of them than in the tongues of the French council; and they should   260 sooner persuade Harry of England than a general petition of monarchs. Here comes your father.

Re-enter the FRENCH KING *and his* QUEEN, BURGUNDY, *and other* Lords

BUR.   God save your majesty! my royal cousin, teach you our princess English?

237–240 *Laissez, . . . seigneur.*] Stop, my lord, stop, stop: on my faith, I don't want you to lessen your greatness by kissing the hand of one of your unworthy servants; excuse me, I beg you, my most powerful lord.

242–243 *Les . . . France.*] It isn't the custom in France for ladies or girls to be kissed before they get married.

248 *entendre . . . moi*] understands better than I.

252 *nice . . . courtesy*] prudish customs curtsy.

253 *weak list*] feeble bounds.

255 *places*] (high) ranks.

K. HEN.   I would have her learn, my fair cousin, how perfectly I
   love her; and that is good English.

BUR.   Is she not apt?

K. HEN.   Our tongue is rough, coz, and my condition is not
   smooth; so that, having neither the voice nor the heart of
   flattery about me, I cannot so conjure up the spirit of love in   270
   her, that he will appear in his true likeness.

BUR.   Pardon the frankness of my mirth, if I answer you for that.
   If you would conjure in her, you must make a circle; if conjure up love in her in his true likeness, he must appear
   naked and blind. Can you blame her then, being a maid yet
   rosed over with the virgin crimson of modesty, if she deny
   the appearance of a naked blind boy in her naked seeing
   self? It were, my lord, a hard condition for a maid to consign
   to.

K. HEN.   Yet they do wink and yield, as love is blind and en-   280
   forces.

BUR.   They are then excused, my lord, when they see not what
   they do.

K. HEN.   Then, good my lord, teach your cousin to consent
   winking.

BUR.   I will wink on her to consent, my lord, if you will teach
   her to know my meaning: for maids, well summered and
   warm kept, are like flies at Bartholomew-tide, blind, though
   they have their eyes; and then they will endure handling,
   which before would not abide looking on.   290

K. HEN.   This moral ties me over to time and a hot summer; and
   so I shall catch the fly, your cousin, in the latter end, and she
   must be blind too.

BUR.   As love is, my lord, before it loves.

K. HEN.   It is so: and you may, some of you, thank love for my
   blindness, who cannot see many a fair French city for one
   fair French maid that stands in my way.

FR. KING.   Yes, my lord, you see them perspectively, the cities
   turned into a maid; for they are all girdled with maiden walls
   that war hath never entered.   300

268 *condition*] personality.
273 *conjure . . . make a circle*] Magicians traced a circle within which they summoned
   the spirits they conjured up to appear. Burgundy turns the reference into one of a
   series of bawdy puns.
276 *rosed over*] blushing.
286 *summered*] nurtured.
288 *Bartholomew-tide*] St. Bartholomew's Day, 24 August (when the flies are sluggish).
298 *perspectively*] as in a perspective glass, which was designed to produce optical illusions.

K. HEN.   Shall Kate be my wife?

FR. KING.   So please you.

K. HEN.   I am content; so the maiden cities you talk of may wait
on her: so the maid that stood in the way for my wish shall
show me the way to my will.

FR. KING.   We have consented to all terms of reason.

K. HEN.   Is 't so, my lords of England?

WEST.   The king hath granted every article:
His daughter first, and then in sequel all,
According to their firm proposed natures.   310

EXE.   Only he hath not yet subscribed this:
Where your majesty demands, that the King of France, hav-
ing any occasion to write for matter of grant, shall name your
highness in this form and with this addition, in French,
Notre très-cher fils Henri, Roi d'Angleterre, Héritier de
France; and thus in Latin, Præclarissimus filius noster
Henricus, Rex Angliæ, et Hæres Franciæ.

FR. KING.   Nor this I have not, brother, so denied,
But your request shall make me let it pass.

K. HEN.   I pray you then, in love and dear alliance,   320
Let that one article rank with the rest;
And thereupon give me your daughter.

FR. KING.   Take her, fair son, and from her blood raise up
Issue to me; that the contending kingdoms
Of France and England, whose very shores look pale
With envy of each other's happiness,
May cease their hatred, and this dear conjunction
Plant neighbourhood and Christian-like accord
In their sweet bosoms, that never war advance
His bleeding sword 'twixt England and fair France.   330

ALL.   Amen!

K. HEN.   Now, welcome, Kate: and bear me witness all,
That here I kiss her as my sovereign queen.

                                    [Flourish.

Q. ISA.   God, the best maker of all marriages,
Combine your hearts in one, your realms in one!

303–305 *I am content . . . my will*] i.e., Henry will forgo demanding in the negotiations
     several French cities in exchange for Katharine.

310 *According . . . natures*] as specified in the proposals.

311 *subscribed*] agreed to.

315–316 *Notre . . . de France*] Our very dear son Henry, king of England, heir of France.

316 *Præclarissimus*] Most renowned. The actual treaty of Troyes calls Henry "præcaris-
     simus," but Shakespeare has copied Holinshed's mistake.

As man and wife, being two, are one in love,
So be there 'twixt your kingdoms such a spousal,
That never may ill office, or fell jealousy,
Which troubles oft the bed of blessed marriage,
Thrust in between the paction of these kingdoms,   340
To make divorce of their incorporate league;
That English may as French, French Englishmen,
Receive each other. God speak this Amen!

ALL.   Amen!

K. HEN.   Prepare we for our marriage: on which day,
My Lord of Burgundy, we'll take your oath,
And all the peers', for surety of our leagues.
Then shall I swear to Kate, and you to me;
And may our oaths well kept and prosperous be!

                           [*Sennet. Exeunt.*

---

337 *spousal*] marriage.
338 *ill office*] unfriendly dealings.
     fell] cruel.
340 *paction*] compact, alliance.
349 *Sennet*] Flourish on trumpets.

EPILOGUE

Enter Chorus

CHORUS.   Thus far, with rough and all-unable pen,
     Our bending author hath pursued the story,
     In little room confining mighty men,
     Mangling by starts the full course of their glory.
     Small time, but in that small most greatly lived
     This star of England: Fortune made his sword;
     By which the world's best garden he achieved,
     And of it left his son imperial lord.
     Henry the Sixth, in infant bands crown'd King
     Of France and England, did this king succeed;   10
     Whose state so many had the managing,
     That they lost France and made his England bleed:
     Which oft our stage hath shown; and, for their sake,
     In your fair minds let this acceptance take.   [*Exit.*

---

2 *bending*] i.e., under the weight of his task.

4 *Mangling by starts*] Distorting by interruptions, by fragmentary treatment.

5 *Small time*] Henry V reigned for only nine years before his death at the age of thirty-five.

7 *the world's best garden*] France.

9 *in infant bands*] in swaddling clothes.

13 *Which oft . . . shown*] a reference to the three parts of *Henry VI* and to the dramatic pieces on which they were based.

14 *let this acceptance take*] let this play meet with your approval.

APPENDIX

ACT III, SCENE IV Translated into English

KATH. Alice, you've been in England, and you speak the language well.

ALICE. A little, madame.

KATH. I beg you, teach me; I've got to learn to speak. How do you say *la main* in English?

ALICE. *La main?* It's called "de hand."

KATH. De hand. And *les doigts?*

ALICE. *Les doigts?* By my faith, I forget *les doigts*. But it'll come to me. *Les doigts?* I think they're called "de fingers." Yes, de fingers.

KATH. *La main*, de hand; *les doigts*, de fingers. I think I'm a very good student; I've learned two words of English so quickly! How do you say *les ongles?*

ALICE. *Les ongles?* We call them "de nails."

KATH. De nails. Listen, and tell me if I'm speaking correctly: de hand, de fingers, and de nails.

ALICE. That's very good, madame. It's excellent English.

KATH. Tell me the English for *le bras*.

ALICE. "De arm," madame.

KATH. And *le coude?*

ALICE. "De elbow."

KATH. De elbow. Now I'm going to repeat all the words you've taught me.

ALICE. I think that will be very difficult, madame.

KATH. Excuse me, Alice. Listen: de hand, de fingers, de nails, de arma, de bilbow.

ALICE. De elbow, madame.

KATH. O my God, I forgot it! De elbow. How do you say *le col?*

ALICE. "De nick," madame.

KATH. De nick. And *le menton?*

ALICE. "De chin."

KATH. De sin. *Le col*, de nick; *le menton*, de sin.